HER BACHELOR COWBOY
BILLIONAIRE

CYNTHIA WOOLF

Published by Firehouse Publishing
Woolf, Cynthia

STAY CONNECTED!

Newsletter

Sign up for my <u>newsletter</u> and get a free book.

Follow Cynthia

https://www.facebook.com/cindy.woolf.5
https://twitter.com/CynthiaWoolf
http://cynthiawoolf.com

Don't forget if you love the book, I'd appreciate it if you could leave a review at the retailer you purchased the book from.

Thanks so much,
Cynthia

CHAPTER 1

*J*essica Kirby sat at the table in her mother's sunny yellow kitchen, trying her best to ignore the woman's words. She was at her mother's for her weekly tea or, in Jessica's case, coffee. Her drink was in her favorite coffee cup.

Sally Kirby was shorter than Jessica by several inches. She sat next to her, wearing a nice day dress with full makeup, earrings, and a necklace. She was only fifty-two and her hair had been blonde ever since Jessica could remember. Now, though, she dyed it to cover the gray coming in, alike between them. Otherwise, Jessica looked exactly like her father, right down to her icy blue eyes. She could always tell when he was happy because his eyes would literally sparkle. And there were times they grew dark when he and her mother were feeling frisky. Of course, Jessica didn't know that then, but she knew it now.

"Jessi, when are you going to get married? I'd like grandchildren before I die."

Jessica rolled her eyes. "You're not dying anytime soon, Mom. You're only fifty-two."

"You don't know that. Your father was only fifty-three when he died, and your Uncle Larry was only forty-nine."

"They were brothers and had bad genes. Grandma Ruby is eighty and still going strong."

Her mother huffed and crossed her arms over her ample chest. "You are twenty-seven years old and not even interested in men now."

Jessica gritted her teeth and had to let her cup go lest she break it. She put her hands in her lap. "It's not that I'm not interested in men. I love men. I write about good men finding good women and living happily ever after. I want that. Do you really think I could write those things if I hated them?" *I write books over and over again about what I dream of. A man sweeping me off my feet. A man that I love and can marry and have children with.*

Her mother leaned over and put an arm around Jessica's shoulders. "My darling daughter, not all men are like Joseph. He was a pig. I told you—"

"Mom, no 'I told you so'. You promised."

"Fine. But you were head over heels for that man and look at you. He's left you a quivering mound of Jell-O. Afraid to try again. Plenty of men out there are like your father. Good, kind men. You just need to find one." She reached into the pocket of her dress and took out a business card. "To that end, I set you up with Mrs. Madison at Love International. She's found you someone already. You'll go on a date to see if you're compatible."

Jessica squinted her eyes shut. "Mom, please." She sat up again. "I don't want to go on a blind date. Wait, a minute. How can she have set me up on a date? I haven't even talked to her."

Sally sat back and rolled her eyes toward the ceiling. "I might have pretended to be you." Then she lowered her gaze back to Jessica's. "Look at it as research for your books. Take a notebook and make notes if you have to. Just make it a small one that will fit inside your evening bag."

"What evening bag? I don't own an evening bag. And why would I need an evening bag?"

"For your first date, of course. I'll loan you one." She sighed, and her lips formed a small smile. "Your father used to take me dancing on Saturday nights, and then sometimes we'd go on a picnic on Sunday afternoon."

Jessica heard the wistfulness in her mother's voice and felt a tug of guilt. "I miss him, too, Mama." She leaned over and hugged her mother.

Sally wiped her eyes with her palms. "Not a day in the last ten years goes by that I don't miss him. We didn't get enough time together. Twenty years was not nearly enough time."

Jessica put her head on her mother's shoulder. "I know, Mama, I know."

She placed her arm around Jessica's shoulders. "Do

this for me, Jessica. I've got a good feeling about this arrangement. Please, just once. Just for me. And if you like the man, all the better, but if you don't, you can decide if you want to try again or not."

Jessica let out a long sigh. "All right, Mama. I'll do it. When do I meet this person?"

Sally squeezed Jessica's shoulders. "Thank you, Jessi. I know you won't regret this. This man will change your life. I know it."

Jessica sat straight and sipped her now-cold coffee. "You don't even know who he is." She turned to her mother and lifted a brow. "Do you?"

Sally looked at the ceiling. "Well, I might have…sort of…maybe taken a peek…" She lifted her arms into the air. "All right, I looked at his profile. His name is Roark Sullivan, and it says he's a corporate executive. He's six feet, two inches, with dark brown hair and green eyes, and he's forty years old."

"Don't you think forty is a bit old for me? A thirteen year age difference—" She didn't really think the age difference was a problem, but if she could convince her mother…

"Might be just perfect. Goodness knows you didn't do well with the men your age. You're too smart for them. They are still little boys. Joseph is a good example. He was happy to spread his—oats, rather than ready himself for married life. Besides, your father was ten years older than me and we had a wonderful marriage."

Jessica stood and paced the kitchen from the double

4

sink to the four-burner gas stove and back. "I try not to think about Joseph and Mandy. They deserved each other...but not to die like they did." *I never told Mom that they were leaving to get married. At least Joseph had been decent enough to send me a letter explaining what they were doing. He even told me to keep the engagement ring... like I would give it back. I'll have it broken down and made into a dinner ring or necklace.*

Sally came close and took her in her arms. "I know, my darling. I try not to think about it, because I am a vengeful person where my daughter is concerned."

She laid her head on her mother's shoulder. "I love you, Mama."

"And I love you, my darling girl. Now, why don't you go home and get ready to go see Mrs. Madison at Love International? She's on the Sixteenth Street Mall in downtown Denver. Just a short walk from your loft in LoDo. Your appointment is at eleven o'clock."

Jessica looked down at her watch. Nine-thirty. *This is not how I planned to spend the day. I'll have to get groceries and gas tomorrow. Hopefully that will be enough time to allot for this Mrs. Madison.* "What do you want me to wear?"

"Your royal-blue top with the sweetheart neckline. And no glasses. I don't know why you insist on wearing them, anyway. It's not like you need them for anything."

She plucked the glasses off and set them on the table. "I started wearing them in the corporate world. I had to do something to get those stupid men to quit hitting on me. I mean, it was like I had a neon sign on my forehead flashing." She opened and closed her hands near her forehead, like a flashing sign. *"Ask me out. Ask me out."* She lowered her hands. "I hated it, so I started wearing no makeup, putting my hair in a bun and wearing those glasses. It worked. The old saying *men don't make passes at girls who wear glasses* is true, thank goodness, and it kept me safe for a while. I guess now it's just habit."

"Well, take them off to meet this Roark Sullivan."

"Yes, Mama. I'll take them off. I need to go now if I'm going to get home in time to make the appointment." She hugged her mother again and left.

I wonder what kind of man I'll meet. Could Mama be right, and I'll meet my other half today?

But she wanted someone to see her as she was every day, not when she's made up to go out dancing. So she wore a turtleneck, *with* her glasses and her hair pulled back. *Let's see if he still wants to date me now.*

ROARK'S CORNER office was on the thirty-second floor of his building. The sun shone in the windows brightly. Even with the tinted windows, he almost felt as if he were outside. He stood behind his mahogany desk and watched his fiancée's beautiful face screw up into a frown before she shrieked.

The tall, thin blonde shot to her feet from one of the matching leather chairs in front of his desk and shook with rage before bursting into tears. "You can't call off the engagement! Our wedding is only a month away."

He stood with his arms to his sides, his hands on the credenza he leaned against. "You should have thought of that before using my London residence for a rendezvous with your lover two weeks ago." He walked over to his desk and glanced at a sheet of paper. "Ben Green. No accounting for taste, I guess."

As suddenly as they started, her tears dried. "I suppose you want your ring back?"

"No, actually, I don't. Sell it. It'll give you and Ben a nice little nest egg."

Meredith picked up her purse and marched to the office door. With her hand on the doorknob, she turned and faced him. "You haven't heard the last of me. Soon you'll come crawling back. After all, we both know you're afraid to be alone." She stormed out the door.

Roark sighed and shook his head. He picked up his cell phone and punched in the numbers. "Trevor, meet me at the club in twenty minutes." Roark listened to his best friend. "I don't care if it's only one-thirty in the afternoon. I need a good stiff drink…and a date for the gala tomorrow night." *Is Meredith right? Am I afraid to be alone? No, I'm not. I just need a date for an event. I can't show up alone, I can't deal with the questions—Where is Meredith? Did something happen? Each of the questions with a snide, all knowing gaze, as if they already know what happened.*

Twenty minutes later, Roark sat in the bar of the Denver Country Club. He sat in a Queen Anne chair upholstered in a gold-colored material with Fleur-de-Lys embroidered on it. Two chairs and a small maple table formed quiet places for talks between members. These intimate settings were places where business deals, marriages and other such arrangements were often made over a snifter of brandy or glass of scotch.

Roark waited impatiently with a glass half full of Wild Turkey 101 bourbon in his hand. *If Trevor doesn't show up soon, they'll have to wheel me on a hand truck to get me to the cab to take me home.* He didn't usually drink much and was upset with himself for letting Meredith's words upset him. Was there truth in them? Is that why he was so angry?

Trevor Howard walked in and sat across from him. The tall, blond man wore a gray business suit. He loosened his tie. "Okay, I've come up with an idea."

Roark smiled. "No—'How are you?' 'What happened?' No sympathy whatsoever?"

Trevor waved a hand in the air, dismissing his light rebuke. "You don't need sympathy; you need congratulations on finally being rid of that bony, gold-digging witch. I thought you were going to do it two weeks ago when you found out she cheated."

Roark chuckled. "You never hold back, do you?" *You've said this to me many times during my relationship with Meredith. Why didn't I listen sooner? I could have saved myself the feigned hysterics and maybe found someone I could really love and not just settle for.*

Trevor grinned. "No. And I never will. That's what you like about me."

The bartender came over, a clean, white cloth folded over his arm. "What can I get for you, Mr. Howard? Your usual?"

"Yes, gin and tonic, Sam. Thanks."

He returned with Trevor's gin and tonic with a lime on the side of the glass. "Enjoy!"

Trevor took a sip, closed his eyes and sighed. "No one makes it quite like Sam and I can't imagine what he does differently, but it's always better than anyplace else. I thought you were getting loose from Meredith two weeks ago when you found out she cheated."

"I was. I didn't get around to it."

"Now that you have *finally* gotten rid of her, I want you to try something different. Your usual way of meeting someone through friends, like you did when I introduced you to Meredith or your mother's friend's granddaughter. They all might have come from wealth, but that doesn't mean they are nice and so far, you haven't had a nice one yet. I don't know how you manage to find the gold digger every time." Trevor shook his head and put up a hand. "Never mind, it doesn't matter. That's all in the past. Your great aunt gave me this information for a matchmaker. A Mrs. Madison at Love International. You only have to do one thing. Go meet her. She requires all her clients to meet her, whether she's found a match for them or not. I've taken care of the rest of it. You're a business execu-tive with no time for the dating rituals. She guarantees her matches the first time round. She says you'll never be disappointed."

Roark shook his head slowly and looked down into his own drink, which was more than half gone. "I don't know. She sounds too good to be true."

"Too bad. I already made the appointment, did the initial questionnaire online and attached your picture from the Kids with Cancer gala last year. Anyway, she's come back with a match. Here she is...Jessica Kirby, romance novelist." He pushed his phone toward Roark. "Definitely not someone I would have picked for you, but what do I know? I introduced you to Meredith."

Roark didn't take the phone. "That's right, you did. Besides, what kind of matchmaker would let you sign up for me?"

"Mrs. Madison's special. I don't know how, but...it was like she was expecting my call and..." Trevor scratched his head and frowned. "I don't understand it myself."

Roark finally took the phone and looked at the screen. The picture was of a woman with dark brown hair, pulled straight back, and icy blue eyes, behind black cat's eye glasses that took up a full third of her face.

She mesmerized Roark. She was beautiful, and he knew she was perfect for him. Meredith was supposed to be his match, but he'd always preferred the bookish type. He wanted an intelligent woman who he could have discussions with about more than what the latest gossip was. He couldn't explain it more than that. He just knew she was for him and suddenly, he couldn't wait to meet her. "When can we get together?"

Trevor lifted his eyebrows, leaned back in the chair and crossed his legs at the knee. "I hadn't expected you to concur so quickly. She's agreed to meet you today for coffee at three o'clock at Starbucks on the Sixteenth Street Mall between Tremont Place and Court Place. She'll be wearing a dark green turtleneck."

Roark chuckled. "She sounds like she's trying to hide her beauty, but I can see through the disguise." He never lifted his eyes from the picture on Trevor's phone. "This one is...special. I just have a feeling. I never felt this way about Meredith or any of my other fiancées. Confirm the meeting. Tell her I'll be wearing a navy blue pinstripe suit." He broke his gaze away from the picture and handed Trevor his phone.

"Well, I certainly hope so. She is the only brunette that you've even been interested in, much less been a fiancée." He typed into his phone and then hit send. "It's done. She'll be at Starbucks in forty-five minutes. That gives you plenty of time to go meet Mrs. Madison and then get to Starbucks, get a coffee, and watch her arrive."

"Given such a short time frame, I wonder if she's eager to meet me or hoping I won't show? I better go." Roark stood and looked down at Trevor, who sat finishing his gin and tonic. "Thanks. I feel good about this."

"I hope it works out. Remember, Mrs. Madison

guarantees her matches, so let's hope she's as good as she says she is." Trevor stood and extended his hand.

Roark took it and then pulled his best friend into a one-armed hug. "I'll call you after the meeting and tell you how it went."

Trevor grinned. "Good. I want to hear all about her."

Releasing Trevor, Roark turned away and hurried out of the club.

Smiling, Roark couldn't wait to meet Jessica Kirby.

* * *

ROARK WALKED INTO LOVE INTERNATIONAL. Behind the computer on the only desk in the room was an elderly woman. "Mrs. Madison?"

She looked up, smiled widely, and then stood. "Mr. Sullivan. Come in. Come in."

The woman had thick, white hair in a braid down her back. She had large gold hoop earrings in her ears and wore a blouse with long puffy sleeves and a high neckline, but the blouse was fitted like she was wearing a corset.

Roark had the feeling that she was…magic. But that was impossible. He was just anxious to get the interview over with.

"You shouldn't be in such a hurry, Roark. May I call you, Roark?"

"Of course."

She opened one of the two doors behind the desk.

It opened into a small conference room, dimly lit with wall sconces that looked like they had candles in them. The table was round and covered with a colorful cloth.

"Come in." She pointed at one of the four chairs at the table. "Sit. Sit."

This was the most unusual setting for a match-maker, though he didn't know what a normal setting was. He expected her to bring out a crystal ball any minute.

She chuckled as she sat across from him. "Now, Roark. Your friend was most forthcoming about your needs and desires, but I've known for a long time that I would meet you. I was waiting for the perfect girl. I guarantee my matches, but I'm sure Trevor told you that or you wouldn't be here."

He was fascinated with her sing-song voice. The sound relaxed him.

She stood and walked to a small stereo system and pressed a button.

Roark hadn't seen a system like that since he was a young man. "Yes, he told me and he showed me the picture you sent of Jessica Kirby. She is beautiful and I don't know why she tries to hide it. Beauty like hers cannot be hidden from those with eyes that see."

"You are quite right. Though the young woman would prefer it most times if those around her saw her for her mind, not her physical self."

"I don't believe one can be separated from the other."

She tilted her head and narrowed her eyes. "Yes, I believe this as well."

"I'm supposed to meet Miss Kirby in less than half an hour."

"Don't worry. We'll finish in plenty of time for you to meet Jessica for coffee."

He forgot for a moment that Mrs. Madison would, of course, know where Jessica wanted to meet. The request had come through the elderly woman. He realized he had no clue how old the woman was. She could have been seventy or one-hundred and seventy. In either case, she was spry for her age.

The woman smiled again, as though she knew what he was thinking. Did she?

"I only have one question for you, Roark. Are you ready to let love into your life? You've spent most of your adult life avoiding it, despite your six fiancées. So, tell me honestly. Are you ready?"

* * *

JESSICA GOT off the Sixteenth Street bus at Tremont Place and walked through the packed sidewalks the half block to Starbucks. The sun was headed down and one side of the street was in shade provided by the tall buildings. Even with the breeze and walking on the shady side, her hands sweated. Maybe wearing a turtle-neck in late August was not the best idea. She wiped her hands on her jeans, took out her phone, and called Lanie. She hoped her hands would still be dry when she met the man. She wanted to shake hands with Roark Sullivan and would be embarrassed if her hands were still sweating.

Lanie answered. "Hi. What's up, girlfriend?"

"I'm on my way to meet a man. A blind date. I really want this to go well, and yet, I'm doing everything to protect myself from him. What's the matter with me?"

"You're just nervous. If he's worth a hoot, he'll see under your disguise for who you are. Besides, you never hide your intelligence and that is attractive, too. You don't want some idiot."

"I don't. I'll just remember I don't have to do anything but have coffee. He can find himself another girl, if that's the case."

"That's right. You've got this. Just be yourself. You'll be fine."

"Thanks, Lanie. You always put things in perspective for me. I love you, my friend."

"I love you, too. Now go get'em."

Jessica laughed and ended the call. Then she looked at the picture Mrs. Madison sent her.

He was a handsome older man. She was eager to meet him, but nervous, too. She'd never dated anyone older than she was. But her dad had been ten years older than her mother, so she didn't think the age gap was that unusual, despite what she'd said to her mother. She just didn't want her mother to be right again.

She walked into the establishment, looked around. The café wasn't that busy, but she didn't see anyone

15

matching the description she had. She ordered her regular drink—a tall, iced, skinny vanilla latte. While she waited for her drink to be prepared, she checked her phone to make sure she had the right place and time. Since she set the place for the meeting, it was a little silly of her to check.

She noticed a couple of men glance at her and then look away. Apparently, her outfit was working. Would it also work on Roark Sullivan?

How could she use this situation in her next book, no matter how this actual date works out? Should she have a matchmaker? Should she make her hero older? Should she have a wallflower and do a Cinderella story? What if he's the Cinderella? She smiled at her thoughts.

When her drink was ready, she sipped it as she found a table in the corner and waited for an older man in a blue pinstripe suit.

Jessica was unprepared for a man to approach her before she'd even taken the second drink of her coffee.

"Jessica Kirby?"

His deep baritone voice washed over me, like caramel syrup over ice cream, sweet and rich. Definitely a line from a romance novel. She smiled and then looked up and up. *He was tall, that's for sure. And more handsome than his picture.* "I'm Jessica Kirby."

He held out a hand. "Roark Sullivan. May I sit?"

She went to take his hand and realized she'd been holding her drink. She wiped her hand on her jeans again, then she smiled. "I didn't think you needed a hand wet from the condensation of my drink. Glad to meet you, Roark. Yes, please sit. Ah, but you haven't gotten a drink yet."

He sat across from her. "I don't need a drink right now."

"All right. Let's talk. What do you want to know about me?" *I want this to go well, but I'm out of practice. I haven't dated anyone since before Joseph and I got together. That was over five years ago. Has dating changed since then?*

"Your profile said you were a romance author. That's an interesting occupation. What kind of romance do you write? Will I have read any of them?"

She took a sip of her drink and then chuckled. "Funny, but I didn't take you for the romance reading type. I'm surprised you know there are different genres of romance. I write historical, contemporary, and scifi romance novels. I doubt you've read any of them."

He shrugged. "Perhaps I have. My mother loves reading romance novels. I've read a few of hers that she recommended to me. How many books to you have out?"

"Thirty-five so far." She took another sip of her drink.

His brows lifted and his deep, emerald-green eyes widened. "That's amazing. How long have you been writing?"

"I started writing full time five years ago, just after college. I wrote some books when I was still in college."

"You're very prolific."

She smiled, delighted she could impress him

already. "Well, they pay the bills and in order to do that, I need to publish consistently. So I publish about nine or ten books a year. When I started, my output was, of course, much less. As I learn more, I get better at writing quickly, and I publish more often."

He leaned toward her, his forearms on the table and his hands clasped. "How can you type that fast?"

She laughed softly, pleased with his interest in her career. "I started dictating a couple of years ago and it tripled my productivity. The learning curve was high, but once I taught the program to recognize my voice and taught it the extra words, I need for my books, it works great. I had to adjust the way I write because I use the words on the page to prompt me for the next words, if that makes sense."

"It does." He sat back. "Would you care to go somewhere for a late lunch or an early dinner? I'd prefer this was a date rather than an inquisition, which it has been. My fault for that. I simply wish to know as much about you as possible."

She took another sip from her straw and wondered why he hadn't said anything about himself. So far, he'd asked all the questions, and she'd answered. Maybe if they went to get something to eat, he would be more forthcoming. "I...I would, and I'd like to know more about you."

He stood and walked behind her to pull her chair out.

"Very chivalrous. Thank you."

He lowered his head in a bow. "You're welcome, my

lady." He straightened and smiled widely. "I have my car close, and I know a great little Mexican restaurant —that is, if you like Mexican food."

Her eyes widened. "It's my favorite." She could almost taste the green chili now.

He grinned. "Mine, too."

She dropped her remaining drink in the trash before leaving Starbucks. "I'm ready when you are." Jessica watched as he put his arm behind her, like he would have guided her with his hand at her waist. But he must have remembered it was their first date and placed his hand behind him instead. Very interesting. He's such a gentleman. I wonder if he always is or just on first dates?

He smiled. "Let's go then. We have a lot to talk about."

CHAPTER 2

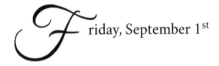riday, September 1ˢᵗ

ROARK WAS glad he'd driven his all-electric Mustang to work that morning. It was less ostentatious than a limo. Jessica didn't seem to know who he was. He didn't know why, but he didn't think his money would matter to her. She just didn't seem the gold digger type, but he'd wait until he knew her better.

He settled her in the car and took off west down Colfax Avenue toward Lakewood. He pulled off into the parking lot for Gordo's Mexican Restaurant. It was his favorite, and he visited them usually once a week. The parking lot was nearly full, but he found an open spot on the back side of the building.

As soon as he walked in, aromas of roasted chilis and fried pork caressed his nose. His mouth watered.

She lifted her chin, closed her eyes, and sniffed the air. Then she opened her eyes and looked at Roark. "It smells wonderful in here."

"Just wait. Your tastebuds are in for a treat."

The owner, Esmeralda Ortega, greeted him, holding several menus. "Ah, Mr. Sullivan. I'm so happy to see you." She waved him down.

He smiled and bent over so the small woman could kiss his cheek. Then he kissed hers in return.

"I'm being rude. You have a young lady with you. Hello, Miss...?"

"Kirby. Jessica Kirby." She held out her hand. "I'm pleased to meet you. Roark has been very complimentary about your establishment and the amazing food. I think he must be correct because you are packed."

Esmeralda shook her hand. "Yes, thankfully we are always busy, but the tables rotate fairly quickly. Also, he's biased. He started coming here as a boy with his papa. My mama was doing the cooking then. Now, I use all of her recipes. The menu has been the same now for forty years. I think, why change it when the customers are happy with it the way it is? When I retire, my daughters, Estrellita and Maria will take over. They already do much of the cooking. I mostly supervise now. But, come. Sit." She waved them into a booth covered in red vinyl. "Let me bring you a drink. What would you like, Miss Jessica?"

"A margarita on the rocks with no salt, please." Jessica looked around. "I love your décor. The paintings of Mexico, the bullfights and lovely moonlit nights are beautiful." She pointed at each painting as she said the words. "I love the use of red in the paintings. Of course, that's my favorite color, so I could be a little biased." She chuckled.

"Thank you, Miss Kirby. My late husband Eduardo painted them."

"He was very talented."

"Thank you for saying so." Esmeralda turned toward Roark. "You want your usual Negra Modelo beer?"

"Yes, please."

"I will be right back with your drinks. In the meantime, you can look over the menu." She handed Jessica one of the menus she held.

It impressed Roark how easily Jessica conversed with Esmeralda, as though they were friends. "I think you'll love the food here. You'll wish they delivered, I guarantee."

Jessica looked over the menu. "I think I'll have the margarita beef burrito."

"Excellent choice. My favorite. I get that, a chili relleno and guacamole salad."

Jessica chuckled. "If I ate like that, I'd blow up like a balloon."

He smiled. "I will have to run a couple of extra miles tomorrow."

"I have a treadmill in my living room. I usually hang my coats on it." She laughed. "I hate working out. I'd rather do something fun. Take a hike, go swimming or to a water park, play miniature golf. I'm not good at the real thing, so I stick to the one with the windmill."

He laughed. He couldn't help himself. She was delightful, with more depth and more grounded than the uber thin women he'd been dating and engaged to. All they were interested in was the latest gossip about what a famous woman was doing now and who she was sleeping with. He can't believe he was ever attracted to those women. Not when compared to Jessica. "I have a question. Why do you wear those glasses? I can tell by looking at you they don't have a prescription in them. So why?"

Her lips curved up, and she blushed. "To keep the men at bay. I get hit on a lot if I don't wear them. This way, they think I'm a geek and don't bother me. I guess that sounds pretty snobbish, doesn't it?"

He leaned on the table with his forearms crossed. "Not at all. I totally understand. I present myself as other than I am. What do you say we tell—or show— each other who we really are?"

The server, Rosa, came to the table with their drinks. She looked like a girl of about fifteen, with black hair in a long braid down her back and dark brown eyes. Roark knew her to be at least ten years older than that. After setting the drinks in front of Roark and Jessica, she took a pad from her apron's pocket.

"What can I get for you, Mr. Sullivan?"

"I'll have my regular, Rosa, and the lady will have the same."

Jessica's eyes widened, and a brow cocked up. "No, the lady will not. I want just the burrito, please, smothered with green chili and cheese."

Rosa wrote on her pad. "Very good. Two margarita beef burritos, one chili relleno crispy and one guacamole salad. I'll be right back with the guac." She hurried away toward the kitchen.

Knowing he'd made a serious faux pas, Roark looked at the table and then up at her. "I'm sorry I overstepped my boundaries. I shouldn't have ordered for you. I just wanted you to try everything I love. I hope you'll forgive me."

She smiled and then shrugged. "It's all right. We have lots of things to learn about each other. One of them is that I like to order for myself."

His lips rolled inward, and he knew he had reddened a bit. "So noted."

Jessica waved her hand and smiled. "Okay. Do you want to go first, as we reveal our real selves?"

He shook his head just slightly. "No, I think mine will take longer to explain."

"All right." She removed her glasses and released her hair from the bun at her nape. She pulled the mass of curls over one shoulder.

The waves fell past the table top but he didn't know how far, just that he'd like to run his hands through those waves and see if it's as silky as it looks.

His eyes widened, and he smiled. "You're even more beautiful than I already thought you were."

She dropped her gaze to the table. "Thank you." She lifted her head and looked directly at him. "Now you."

He took a deep breath and let it out. "As you know, my name is Roark Sullivan. I'm the owner and CEO of Sullivan International Holding Co."

Her brows furrowed a little. "I'm sure I'm supposed to know who you are from that, but I don't. I'm afraid I don't even own a TV or keep up with either the stock market or the gossip rags."

He waved her words away. "It's probably better that you don't or you would have seen and heard a lot of gossip about me. All of it was overblown. I simply request fidelity of my fiancées, and thus far no one has provided it. The last one used my London home for her rendezvous'."

Jessica covered her mouth but burst out laughing, anyway. "Your London house. Oh, my God. That's rich." She laughed harder. "I'm sorry. I shouldn't laugh at your expense."

He chuckled and then began to laugh, and soon he was laughing as hard as she was. Roark hadn't felt this at ease with someone, especially a woman, in ages. Maybe ever.

"How many fiancées have you had?"

He reached over and took her hand in his. "Too many. My mother wants me to marry and have an heir." He pulled his hand away and leaned back in the booth. "I've been engaged six times. Meredith Vandermeer was the most recent. For some reason, I can't get a woman who is faithful. What does that say for me?"

He realized if he moved too fast, he could scare her away. "Jessica, I have an engagement coming up and need a date. Would you consider going with me to the Kids with Cancer fundraiser and ball tomorrow? I know it's the Saturday before Labor Day, but if you don't have something planned..."

She lifted both brows and her lips forms an _O_. "Actually...I'd love to attend the gala with you. I go every year anyway. Well, to the auction. I've never stayed for the ball." _This could be good info for my next contemporary. What happens at the dance? I've never known._

He leaned back toward the table and held his right hand palm up on the table. He waited for her to put her hand in his.

When she did, he wanted to shout to the rafters and jump for joy, but he stayed calm. "This time, you'll stay for the ball. I promise you'll have a good time."

Rosa brought their food, and the conversation stopped.

Jessica took a bite of her burrito, chewed, and swallowed. "This is wonderful. I love the green chili. It's not too hot but is still very flavorful. I dislike green chili that makes my forehead sweat. It's so unattractive when your makeup runs onto your food." She laughed.

He chuckled and then took a bite of his relleno and chewed. The cheese melted in his mouth, and the mild green chili was perfect when combined with the crispy outer shell. Rellenos need to be eaten when they are hot and the cheese is melty. He finished his bite and chuckled. "I knew you'd love this place. I've never brought anyone else here."

She frowned. "Why not? The food is great."

He shrugged. "It's not fancy enough for the women I usually date." *For all the good it's done me.* "But you're different. You're real. I mean, you're down-to-earth."

Jessica shrugged. "I am who I am. I never learned to be fake about anything important, just the disguise." She lifted her arms and spread them wide. "This is me." She rested her left forearm on the table and picked up her fork with her right hand.

He reached over and placed his right hand on her left one, where it lay on the table. "I like what I see. You're honest, except for your little disguise, and I don't blame you. I'd definitely ask you out."

She pulled her hand back and set it in her lap, all the while blushing and looking down at her plate.

He picked up his fork. "I'm sorry. I don't mean to push. I've just never met anyone like you. Thank you for agreeing to come with me to the gala. I wasn't looking forward to it before, and now I find I can't wait for tomorrow."

She smiled. "You're a funny man. Some people would say you have it all, and would trade places in a heartbeat, but I see someone who is just like everyone else, with problems and fears and hurts."

He blotted his mouth with a napkin. "I didn't think I was so transparent. I'm not sure I want you to see so far inside me so soon."

Jessica swallowed her food and took a drink from

her margarita. "You're not transparent. I like to see below the surface, and the man I'm seeing there is much more interesting than the man the world sees."

Hearing her words made him lean back into the booth. "How can you know that? I don't usually let anyone see below the surface, so to speak. Even now."

"I wouldn't say that." She looked around them and waved a hand above her head in a circle. "You brought me to your favorite restaurant to see if I'd turn my nose up. You didn't know Mexican food is my favorite, but you were pleased you'd made an excellent decision, *and* my reaction surprised you."

He rested against the back of the booth and placed an arm along the top. "That's true. I was, I am. You're not at all what I expected. That's the reason I asked you to the gala tomorrow."

"And you're not what I expected of *the* Roark Sullivan, which is why I agreed to go with you." She took another bite of her burrito. "Oh, my God, this is so good."

Roark liked seeing a woman enjoy her food. He was tired of the stick-thin models he'd been dating—and even engaged to. They ordered lobster, ate two bites, and *simply couldn't eat another bite* but took the leftovers home, supposedly for the dog. Meredith hadn't even owned a dog.

What was the matter with him? Why had he even considered those women? He didn't like them and certainly didn't love them.

His great aunt and his mother badgered him about

leaving an heir, so he was intent on marrying to have a child. But most of the women he'd chosen hadn't wanted a child. They didn't want to ruin their figures with pregnancy. "How do you feel about kids?"

She lifted her brows and leaned forward. "You get right to it, don't you?" Moving back, she picked up her fork and cut a bite of burrito. "That's all right. Usually, if I remember correctly, that's a fourth or fifth date question, but it doesn't matter. I'm in favor of children. I want four." She put the burrito in her mouth.

He widened his eyes and, interest piqued, he listened. "Four! Why four? I had thought about two."

She shrugged and swallowed. "Well, I'm an only child and didn't like it. I always wished I had siblings."

Roark leaned forward and put his forearms on either side of his plate. *I'm being too forward. I'm assuming we will be a couple. I shouldn't assume anything, not with Jessica. She's too important.* "I have two brothers and we were always fighting as kids. Are you sure you want to deal with that?"

She nodded. "And what about now? How do you get along?"

"We're best friends."

Another server, a young woman with her long, black hair tied back in a low ponytail, came by the table. "Are you folks finished?"

"Yes, thank you," said Roark.

"Yes. Tell the chef it was the best food I've had in a very long time," said Jessica.

CYNTHIA WOOLF

"I'll do that. She will be pleased." She picked up the empty dishes and left.

"Now, how about you?" Jessica leaned forward again and crossed her arms in front of her on the table. "Just two kids? I still vote for lots of kids."

He shook his head and laughed. "Look at us. Talking like we're getting married tomorrow. How about we leave this conversation for another date? Maybe the fourth or fifth?"

She took a sip of her margarita. "You've got a deal… if we have a fourth or fifth date."

He narrowed his eyes a little and then opened them again. "Oh, we will, I guarantee it." He smiled and winked.

She held firm. "We'll see if we can get through the gala and then go from there."

"Very well. Shall we go? I could stay and talk to you all night, but I think they need the table."

"Of course." She slid from the booth.

He was out before her and held his hand out to her.

She stood, looked down at his hand, and took it.

He was afraid she wouldn't, but was glad she proved him wrong.

They walked hand in hand out to the car, where he opened her door for her and waited for her to get in and buckle up before he closed the door. Then he went around the car and climbed into the driver's side.

After putting on his seat belt, Roark pressed the ignition button, and the car came to life. "Where to now?"

"Home please. I have appointments to go to before tomorrow night, beginning tonight." She gave him her address.

"I would protest, but I know I'm seeing you for the gala tomorrow, so I'll be patient." He pulled out of the parking lot, headed south to Sixth Avenue, and then drove east back into Denver.

She chuckled. "You're certainly easily entertained. One dinner and a promise to go with you to the gala and you're happy."

Roark gazed at her. "Not happy, but content to wait while you decide you like me."

"I'm going to the gala. Beyond that, I can't say."

He looked over at her and grinned, then returned his gaze toward the street. "But you've not ruled anything out."

"Not yet."

He pulled up in front of her building and turned off the ignition. Then he angled his body toward her. "May I walk you to your door?"

"Yes, I'd like that."

Roark got out of the Mustang and came around to her side. He opened her door and extended his hand to her.

She grasped it and stepped out of the car. Holding her clutch with one hand, she dug into it for her keys. When they reached the door, she put in the code and then walked down the hall to her loft. She unlocked the door and opened it.

"Would you like to come in for a nightcap?"

He wanted to, very much, but he also wanted her to want him. "I think I'll call it a night. I've got some things to do tomorrow, as well. I'll pick you up at seven, if that meets with your approval."

"Oh, all right. Yes, seven would be good. I'll see you tomorrow night, then."

"Yes, goodnight."

She went into the loft.

Roark waited until he heard the door's deadbolt engage before he returned to the car. He started it and pulled away from the curb.

He pressed a button on the video screen. "Call Veronica."

An image appeared of a beautiful woman with flaming red hair, straight and cut in a razor-sharp chin-length bob. "Roark. Darling. How are you?"

"Hello, Veronica. I need you to do something for me. I need a dress, specifically the red gown I saw in your showroom on Monday."

She continued. "Darling, you've always had such exquisite taste. What size is the woman this time? Zero or a three maybe?"

He smiled. "You sound tired of those women." He certainly was.

"Oh, dearest, I wish you'd tire of them and find a real woman. Those models are skin and bones, literally. I could see her spine and her ribs on that last one you sent over. I want to dress a real woman, with curves, hips and breasts."

He looked behind him for traffic and then smoothly

blended in with the southbound traffic on I-25. "Well, you'll have your chance. I want that red gown in your size, sent to this address tonight, along with a suitable coat."

She tsked. "You don't cover a dress like that with a coat. A fur stole or lace shawl would be perfect."

Roark shook his head. "No fur, but the lace will work. The address is 1801 Market Street, Loft 1B. Miss Jessica Kirby."

"All right, I'll send it. This one will set you back some. It's the most beautiful creation I've ever made. It's fifty-thousand dollars. I never actually expected it to sell. It was more artwork than clothing. The gems on the bodice are worth forty-thousand on their own."

"I don't care what the cost is. I want her to have that dress, but you are never to tell her or anyone else its cost. Ever."

"Whatever you say, my darling, Roark."

"I mean it, Veronica. For her safety, no one can know the dress's value." *Jessica would be embarrassed and uncomfortable if she knew the value of the dress and I won't do that to her.*

She nodded with her eyebrows raised. "I understand. No one here knows the value of the dress. Only you and I do. I promise I will tell no one."

"Good. Thank you. I'll talk to you soon. End call." His screen went back to showing the map of the direction home.

He smiled, remembering how funny she was as well as beautiful. He couldn't wait for tomorrow night.

CHAPTER 3

*J*essica closed her door and turned the deadbolt. It surprised her Roark didn't want to come in. Oh, well, she'd have that much more time to look through her dresses for the one to wear tomorrow night.

She loved her loft. It had taken all her savings, but she'd bought it free and clear. She walked through her living room with its floor-to-ceiling windows that became opaque at the touch of a button. She loved her view of the Platte River and, if she got to the far left on her patio, of the mountains. From there, she walked through her kitchen. She'd chosen black appliances to go with the black granite counters with the gold specks that looked like stars. Then she had a butler's pantry, which she'd turned into a wine bar, then her bedroom.

She'd splurged when she'd moved in and gotten a gorgeous bedroom suite from Woodley's. The eight-drawer bureau with attached mirror, chest of drawers, nightstands, queen-size headboard and footboard were all dark cherry wood. She'd also gotten a cheval mirror also in cherry wood.

In the walk-in closet, she kicked her shoes off and pulled out all her old prom and bridesmaid dresses, every sparkly gown she had, and laid them on the bed. The longer she looked at them, the more nauseous she felt. They were horrible. No way could she wear something like that to the gala with Roark.

She picked up her phone and punched Lanie's number.

"Get your bottom over here, now. I need help."

"Not even a 'hi'?"

"It's an emergency. I have a date for tomorrow night's Kids with Cancer fundraiser gala."

"So? You go to that every year."

"Not with Roark Sullivan, I don't."

Lanie was silent for a moment. "*The* Roark Sullivan?" she whispered. "Of Sullivan International Holding Co.? *That* Roark Sullivan?"

"Yes, now get over here."

Twenty minutes later, the doorbell rang.

Jessica ran for the door from the bedroom and opened the door.

Lanie stood on the threshold. She wore her long black hair in cornrows to the back of her head and then gathered into a long braid down her back. She always looked beautiful. She wore a pale peach-colored top that made her caramel skin glow. Her earrings were gold hoops in three sizes, with the largest in the lobe and the smallest on the top of her ear.

Jessica hugged her friend. "I'm so glad you're here. I'm in trouble."

"Why?"

"I don't have anything to wear to a formal gala. I never go to the ball, just the auction. Come look." She hurried into her bedroom.

All over the bed were glittering, sparkling, sequin-laden dresses and gowns.

"These are all my formals, and none of them say sophistication. They all say," she used finger quotes, "high school."

Lanie crossed her stomach with her left arm. Then she held her right elbow in her left palm and put a finger on her chin. "Maybe not. Let's look at them again. To start toss out all the short ones. You are not wearing a mini dress to the gala. I don't care how good your legs are."

Jessica put those to one side of the queen-sized bed.

"Now, let's see." Lanie ran a hand over the satin bodice of the blue sequined gown with cap sleeves. She shook her head. "Girl, that was ugly when you wore it the first time."

Jessica shrugged. "Jenny loved it, and it was her wedding."

Lanie cocked one brow. "And look where that lack of taste got her. She's on her third marriage in six years."

Jessica sighed. "I know."

"What else do you have?" Lanie stood with her hands on her hips.

Pulling a pink satin number from the pile, Jessica held it up against her front. "What do you think?"

Lanie waved her hands in front of her. "No. Just no! You'll look like a walking bottle of Pepto-Bismol."

"Here's one. You can't have any problems with this one." Jessica held up a lavender dress with chiffon over a silk sheath.

Lanie placed her hands back on her hips. "Yeah, no problems at all, if you're mother of the bride."

Jessica unzipped the dress and let it pool in a puddle at her feet.

The doorbell sounded.

"Would you get that, please? I really don't feel like flashing anyone."

"Sure." Lanie headed to the front door. She returned a few minutes later carrying a large, flat box.

Jessica had put on her bathrobe. Her brows went up as she walked toward Lanie and pointed. "What's that?"

Lanie's brows were up and her eyes were wide. "I don't know, but it's from Veronica Sattler's House of Design."

Jessica shook her head but took the box from Lanie. "He couldn't. He doesn't know my size."

"Open it and let's see what it looks like."

Jessica set the box on the bed and lifted off the top, then folded back the tissue paper. A red silk dress with jewels sewn into the bodice lay nestled inside. "Oh, my God, Lanie." She pulled the dress from the box and held it up to her body. "It looks...perfect."

Lanie threw all the dresses to one side of the bed and then sat waving her hands at the dress. "Try it on. Quick, before I try it on for you."

She nodded and shucked her robe, which left her in nothing except her panties. Next, she unzipped the dress, stepped into it, and pulled the strapless gown up and over her breasts. "Zip me up, please." The zipper brought the sides together, and then she adjusted her bosom so it was comfortable in the dress. She ran her hands down the gown, loving the feel of the silk against her skin. She walked over to the cheval mirror, the dress swinging around her ankles. It was the perfect dress for dancing. With her four-inch black heels, it would be the perfect length. Jessica finally turned toward Lanie. "Well, what do you think? I'll wear my hair down and make sure it isn't unruly, but just wavy. Tell me what you see. Don't just sit there with your mouth open."

"It's gorgeous and totally beautiful. It's like they made the dress just for you. How could he do that with only one meeting?"

She turned her back to the mirror and looked over her shoulder to see. "Well, it was a nice date." *Wow! It even looks great from behind. I figured sitting all the time, I had gotten flabby, but I'm not.*

Lanie stood and walked over to Jessica. She circled her looking at every side. "You'll need to keep your makeup neutral and let the dress do all the talking. Are you meeting him there, or is he picking you up?"

"I don't know. He didn't say."

Lanie sat back on the bed and crossed her black-spandex clad legs. Her voice took on a dreamy quality. "I bet he'll bring the limo and pick you up, then you can make an entrance together."

Lanie was always put together. The long peach top, black leggings and black suede three-inch heels looked great on her graceful body. She wasn't skin and bones, just svelte, with curves in the right places.

Jessica was never put together. She always looked a little like she'd just jumped out of a tornado. Even her taste in clothes was bad. Look at all the dresses she owned. Dresses she'd worn to weddings and prom. Why did she still have them? They were so out of style; she didn't think they would even make decent Halloween costumes. "I suppose. I'd rather drive myself, then I can leave whenever I want."

"Tell him your concerns. Maybe he's a reasonable man."

"He is. Almost too reasonable. He didn't kiss me goodnight or come in for a nightcap. Said he had some things to do. Now, I know what. It is beautiful, isn't it?" She swayed in half circles, letting the dress swing at the bottom. She felt like a princess. "But should I accept the gift and wear it?"

Lanie jumped up from the bed and hurried over to Jessica. "Of course. Are you crazy? You want to wear one of those things?" She pointed at the hideous dresses on the bed. "You should give all of them to charity for Halloween costumes. You'd wear one of those, rather than this magnificent gown he sent you? Have you lost your mind entirely?"

Jessica started to sit and then remembered the dress and decided if she would not keep it, she should do her best not to wrinkle it. "You know, I didn't even know who he was. Even when I first heard his name, I didn't put two and two together. Who would have thought Roark Sullivan would use a matchmaker?"

Lanie's eyes widened and her eyebrows shot up nearly to her hairline. "You met him through a matchmaker? I want her name."

"Mrs. Madison at Love International. She's down on the Mall. Mom made the appointment for me. She's a really sweet old lady. Her gold hoop earrings and peasant blouse made me think of...never mind. It's silly."

"What? Tell me."

Jessica walked over to the window, opened the blinds, and looked out. "She almost seemed to be an old Romany woman. Full of magic. How's that for a romance writer? But this whole thing has seemed magical." Forgetting the dress, she sat on the bed and put her face in her hands, then ran her hands back through her hair. "What's wrong with me, Lanie? Am I so lonely that I'm imagining things now? Do I just want to believe that Roark is interested in me because he sent me a beautiful dress and asked me to a ball? This could all be because he needed a date."

"And he went to a matchmaker to find a date? Even I don't believe that, and you know how skeptical I can be. Besides, I want to know if he has a best friend for your best friend?"

"I don't know. That's the point. I don't know much about him...at least yet. He's so nice and so handsome." She put her hands on the bed behind her and raised her face toward the ceiling, and closed her eyes. She remembered how his voice covered her like a soft caress. "I can't figure out why he'd be interested in someone like me."

Lanie rolled her eyes. "You're beautiful. You also happen to be funny, smart, down-to-earth and sensible, besides. What's not to like? And when he discovers you can dance like Ginger Rogers, he'll be in love."

She took a deep breath. "Okay, whatever the reason, I like him, too. And I really want to go to the gala tomorrow night. But I need some jewelry...don't I?"

Lanie shook her head. "No, my darling friend. The dress has its own jewels and they are beautiful. They sparkle almost like they were real, but that can't be... can it?" Her eyes widened as she jutted her chin toward the dress.

Jessica looked down at the bodice of the gown. Small stones—diamonds, emeralds, and sapphires— dotted the entire bodice, sparkling with every move she made. "I don't know, but I'm treating the dress like they are. I don't want anything to happen to this gown."

"Look, sweetie, it's late, at least for me. I have to work from four a.m. until noon. I'm going home and

41

try to get some sleep. I'm going to pretend I'm Cinderella and dream about my own Prince Charming. You have fun tomorrow night, and don't worry about the dress or anything else but having a good time. This is a once-in-a-lifetime opportunity. Grab that brass ring and go for it. But be cautious, too. The man has had six fiancées in the last four years." She hugged Jessica. "I love you, girlfriend."

"I love you, too." She walked Lanie to the door. "I'll call you tomorrow night."

"You better." Lanie headed down the hallway.

After watching Lanie go outside, Jessica closed and locked her front door, then she leaned against it. She ran her hands down her body, admiring the soft feel of the silk. She felt like Cinderella and suddenly wondered when she'd lose her glass slipper.

* * *

SATURDAY EVENING CAME and Jessica had taken more than an hour-and-a-half to make it seem like her look was effortless. Her hair was naturally wavy, but she still curled the ends under so they'd look finished.

Her makeup comprised a dewy foundation, neutral lipstick with a light pink gloss over it and neutral eyeshadow with mascara, lots of mascara. She wanted to look like she had thick, long lashes. She'd even taken the time to groom her eyebrows.

When she was out with her mother that day, shopping for her grandmother's birthday present, she'd splurged on a jeweled evening clutch. In it, she put a lip gloss, her loft key, one-hundred dollars in cash, and a credit card for her donation.

She checked herself again in the cheval mirror to make sure everything was tucked in and she wouldn't flash anyone.

A knock sounded from the front door.

Jessica hurried to the door, took a moment to catch her breath, and then opened it. She should have taken longer with her breathing because, looking at Roark in his tux, she was suddenly breathless.

"You look great." She blurted the words before she could stop herself.

He chuckled. "I'm glad I meet your approval." He looked her up and down. "I must say, the dress looks much better on you than on Veronica's mannequin."

Her face heated, and she lowered her gaze. "It's the most beautiful gown I've ever seen and," she raised her gaze to meet his. Suddenly, she knew that thanking him was enough. "Thank you."

"You're welcome." He smiled. "I have something for you."

His already deep voice seemed even deeper. She stepped toward him. "Oh, Roark, how can I accept anything more from you?"

"You have to. It goes with the dress. It wasn't finished last night, so I picked it up on the way here." He handed her a box about a foot square and not even half an inch thick.

"All right. Please come in." She was glad she'd

cleaned up. She even took the clothes off the treadmill. She walked over to the sofa and set her clutch on the coffee table. Then she removed the top of the box and put it on the table. Inside was the most exquisite, delicate, black lace shawl she'd ever seen. "Oh, my goodness. This is fabulous and perfect for this dress." After picking it up, she let it fall open and then placed it around her shoulders. She turned toward Roark. "How do I look?"

"Beautiful. I knew it was perfect for you. Are you ready to go? I can't wait to show you off."

I'm not exactly happy to be shone off. It feels strange to have people, men in particular, look at me like I'm a piece of meat. Then again, maybe I'm making too big a deal about this. It will be worth it to be with Roark. I like him a lot... maybe too soon and too much. "I am." She grabbed her clutch off the coffee table and headed to the door.

Roark followed.

She closed it behind them and locked the deadbolt with her key, then she replaced the key in her clutch.

He held out his arm.

She placed her hand into the crook of his elbow and walked out of the building at his side.

Outside, parked at the curb, was a white stretch limousine. *I've never ridden in a limo before. I've only seen the inside in movies.*

The driver already held the door open. "Good evening, Miss Kirby."

"Um, good evening to you." *I'm not used to being addressed by someone I've never met before.*

Jessica stepped into the vehicle and slid on the soft leather seat to the other side of the car.

"Mr. Sullivan." The driver nodded his head slightly toward Roark.

"Thank you, George."

Roark climbed into the car.

The driver closed the door after him.

Jessica gazed around the inside of the limo. The seats were the softest leather she'd ever felt. Across from her, the seat had a middle table, which held a decanter of what dark liquid she assumed was brandy. The carpet under her feet was nicer than the carpet in her loft.

"I must insist you put on your seat belt, my dear."

"Oh, of course." She quickly buckled the belt, though she hated the thought it would leave a crease. But that was better than the alternative if they should get into an accident. "So far, this has been the most amazing evening of my life. Thank you, Roark."

The car pulled away from the curb and she could barely feel it move. The ride was so smooth.

"It's my pleasure, Jessica." He lifted her hand and brought it to his lips. He kissed the top, then turned it over and kissed the middle of the palm and then her wrist.

She shivered. Just these little touches, and she was already more turned on than she'd ever been. She was literally putty in his hands.

He didn't release her hand, but tilted his head down a little. "I read in your profile that you volunteer with the Boys and Girls Club and you're twenty-seven. Jessica, does the age difference between us bother you?"

She smiled. "Not in the least. My father was ten years older than my mother, and I swear to you, she was the adult in their relationship. My father was a nice, cheerful man. He loved to laugh and loved to make people laugh. But he didn't take care of himself and that, along with heredity, killed him long before it should have." Her throat tightened as she spoke of her father's death. She closed her eyes, not wanting to relive the pain she felt then.

"I'm sorry to hear that. I assure you I take care of myself and I have no hereditary conditions. Nothing to worry about in that arena."

"I'm glad to hear it."

He finally released her hand. "Tell me, what book are you working on now? I read your latest book today."

She thought for a minute. "You read my latest historical romance, A Heart of Silver, correct? Thank you for reading my book. I have to ask. Did you like it?"

He lifted her hand and kissed it again. "I did. You have quite the imagination. Who would have thought of angels coming back to Earth to save a deserving man and grant his heart wish?"

She grinned. "I was feeling divinely inspired for that series of books. What do you do for fun? Do you take any time for vacations?"

"I definitely take time off. Though, I'm not sure it would be called a vacation. I go to Montana, to my ranch there. It's where I'm happiest. I work with the cattle, go camping and fishing."

She pressed her hands into her lap and turned her body toward him before she realized she was emphasizing her bosom and quickly sat back. "Oh, I love to camp and fish. I haven't gone in years, not since my father died." She took a deep breath and let it out over the lump in her throat. "I miss it. I miss him."

Roark took both of her hands in his. "Why don't you come with me to Montana? We can go camping and I'll show you the best fly-fishing water in the state."

She wanted to say *yes* so badly. "I don't know. I'm on deadline and my editor is expecting 100 pages within the week."

He didn't release her hands, but rubbed circles on the top with his thumbs. "Think about it. I'm planning to go for a week and I'm leaving early next Friday."

"I will…think about it. It's a very tempting offer." If she did what her heart wanted, she would go, no questions asked. She was more attracted to Roark than any man she'd ever known.

But her head said for her to slow down and think about what he was really asking. Did he expect sex while they were at his ranch, probably out in the middle of Nowhere, Montana?

And what about her book? She needed to finish it and get it to her editor.

He pulled her as close as he could while she wore a

seatbelt. "What do you need in order to work from my ranch?"

She watched him in the dim lights of the interior of the limo. He was anxious, even worried she'd say no. Seeing him this way was strange to her and probably to him. She doubted he'd ever had a woman turn him down for anything. "Basically, all I need is a wi-fi signal and a place to put my computer."

"I have those at the ranch. There is a desk in the sitting area of the bedroom you would occupy."

She pulled her hand back. "I still have to think about it. I'm not giving you an answer off the top of my head."

He sat back with a smile. "But you are thinking about it. That's all I can hope for."

The limo arrived at the convention center, where the driver pulled to the curb and let them out in front.

Roark offered his hand to help her out of the car.

Given her four inch-heel heels and the weight of the silk dress, she was grateful for his strength assisting her.

Again, he held out his left arm.

The evening was still warm, and she was glad she didn't have anything heavier than the lace shawl. She took his arm and walked with him into the center.

Lights flashed as they walked the red carpet to the middle of the five sets of double doors into the convention center. A reporter tried to get Roark's attention, but he ignored her.

Once inside, Roark seemed to know everyone.

The men raised their brows and eyed her up and down like they were removing her clothes.

The women also looked at her dress.

Jessica saw them putting dollar signs on it.

She didn't care about either. All she cared about was being with the man who'd brought her. And thinking about the exciting proposition he'd made.

Now what would she do? Follow her heart? Or her head?

CHAPTER 4

*R*oark walked straight through the crowd to the dance floor and took Jessica into his arms, dancing to a slow song.

He smelled her perfume when they embraced, and it hit him like a love potion. "I've wanted to get you in my arms since you opened the door to your loft." He pulled her just a little closer.

She wrapped her arms around his neck and smiled up at him. "I feel good in your arms. Like I belong here. Is that crazy or what?"

"It's not crazy, Jessica. It just means we were made to be together. I don't pretend to know how or why, but it just is. I can feel it."

"So you feel it, too? I don't want to be a plaything, Roark. You've had six fiancées. That doesn't bode well for us, as your reputation precedes you in matters of the heart. You appear as ruthless in love as in business."

"You're no one's plaything, Jessica, least of all mine.

I will never treat you as such and if I do, you have my permission to bean me with a cast-iron skillet to get my attention."

She laughed.

With her laugh, he felt lighthearted, something he hadn't felt for a long, long time.

The music changed to a tango, and she followed him perfectly, even when he dipped her. She didn't stiffen but trusted him, and they moved flawlessly with the music.

When the dance was over, he led her off the floor. They were both breathing a little hard.

She fanned herself with a hand. "That was fun. I haven't danced for a long time, but I need something to drink."

"You dance beautifully. Did you take lessons for one of your books?"

"Ding, ding, ding." She looked at him and tapped the end of her nose. "Go to the head of the class. Yes, one of my historical stories required my learning to dance. I'm surprised I remembered. What about you? When did you start dance lessons?"

"I began lessons when I was a teenager, about fourteen, I think. My mother was determined that all of us have some sophistication and thought dance lessons were a good place to start. I can't say that I disagree with her." He leaned down and whispered in her ear. "Those lessons let me hold you close, so to me, every session was worth it." He straightened. "Let me get us some champagne." He walked away and left her on her own. He wanted to see how she interacted without him.

* * *

"So you're the witch he threw me aside for."

Jessica turned toward the voice and gazed at a woman with icy platinum blonde hair in a silver lamé dress that emphasized her thin body.

"I don't have any idea who you are or what you're talking about." She looked over the woman's head, searching for Roark.

The blonde lifted her chin and tried to look down her nose at Jessica, even though she was shorter. "I'm Meredith Valkenburg. I was his fiancé until yesterday morning."

Jessica cocked a brow and gazed at the woman again. *Yesterday! Roark only broke up with her yesterday. I thought it had been some time ago. I had no idea that Meredith had treated him dirty such a short time ago.* "I heard about you. Perhaps you shouldn't have cheated."

Meredith's nostrils flared and her perfect eyebrows formed slashes over her narrowed eyes. "You don't have any idea what I put up with. He deserved what he got."

For a moment, Jessica wondered what the woman meant. *Was she trying to warn me about Roark?* Jessica decided whatever had happened was between them and she was determined to leave it there. "And you might have deserved what you got as well. Now, please go away. You're ruining my evening."

The woman suddenly narrowed her eyes, parted her lips in a snarl, and slapped Jessica across the face.

Jessica's mouth opened and, astonished at what had just happened, she put her left hand against her cheek. With the greatest restraint she'd ever shown, she turned fully toward Meredith, her eyes narrowed. "Are you done? I suggest you leave now, before I have security call the police so I can press charges for assault. These nice people all saw you strike me, unprovoked."

ROARK APPEARED at Jessica's side along with a tall, blond man, also in a tux. "Jessica! Are you all right?" He looked at her and cupped her hand as it lay on her cheek. "I'm sorry. I'll take care of this." He turned to the blonde woman, and could barely keep his anger in check. She'd hurt Jessica, and all he wanted was to hurt her in return. His instinct was to protect Jessica. Roark had to tamp those inclinations down. "What do you want here, Meredith?" He placed an arm around Jessica's waist and drew her close.

"I wanted to see the little witch that you put me aside for." She spat the words.

"I 'put you aside,' as you say, before I'd even met Jessica. I received pictures of you and your boyfriend leaving my London home two weeks ago. I should have called off our engagement then, but I waited until you made your demand to have the wedding in Rome, which I also know that Ben Green put you up to.

"Did you really think I don't keep track of what goes on at my homes? Did you think paying off the caretaker was enough? I have security cameras in almost every room in my homes. If I'm not in residence, I always turn the cameras on. I fired the caretaker, by the way, because he took your bribe. I could tell you what I think of you, but this is not a place for such language. As for Jessica, even knowing her for just one day, I've learned what a genuine lady is like. *You* are not one."

"Why you—"

Roark's body literally shook, and he fisted his hands. "Trevor, please escort Meredith away from here."

The blond man stepped forward and put his arm around the woman's shoulders. "Now, Meredith, come with me and tell me all about it. Let's leave them be." He guided the blonde away.

Jessica watched them go and finally lowered her hand from her stinging cheek.

Roark turned, so Jessica was in front of him. He put his hands on her upper arms. "I am sorry she directed her contempt at you. She's being unfair, and you and I both know that."

JESSICA RAISED her gaze to his face as butterflies were suddenly flying fighter jets in her stomach. *Have I gone on a date with an engaged man? Did I just do to that woman what Mandy did to me?* "Are you sure you didn't meet me until after you'd—"

His mouth turned up on one side. "I'm sure. I hadn't even talked to Mrs. Madison until just before lunch. It shocked me when she told me she had someone for me already."

"That is amazing." *Do I believe him? Did he really meet me after?*

"I call it kismet. You were meant for me. I mean, we are meant to be together. Don't you feel it?"

She lowered her gaze as a shiver ran up her spine. "You're right I do. I just needed to hear it again."

He snagged two glasses of champagne from a passing server and handed her one. "Drink your champagne." He leaned down and whispered conspiratorially. "It's the one wine I didn't supply. This is champagne from France. I insisted if they were determined to serve champagne, that it be real and not just sparkling wine."

Jessica wondered if he was more than just an attendee and wine supplier to the gala. Otherwise, what would give him the right to tell them what wine or champagne is served? She lifted the glass to her lips and noticed her hand was shaking, but she took a sip.

Roark emptied his glass and set it on the tray of another passing server. Then he took her hand in his. "What do you say we get out of here?"

"I haven't given my donation yet."

"I'll make sure they get them both tomorrow. In the meantime, I've got something to show you."

Why does he want to leave the gala so soon after getting here? Is he ashamed of me? Should I have physically defended myself?

She finished her drink.

Roark took her glass in one hand and placed his other hand at her waist. He saw another server and set the glass on his empty tray. Then he easily guided her out of the convention center while calling for his car on the phone.

A few people tried to get him to stop and talk, but he simply looked at them, lifted a brow, and they moved along.

When she and Roark arrived outside, the limo was by the curb, and George stood beside the back door. As they approached, he opened it.

Roark helped Jessica into the car and then followed her. "Thank you, George. Take us home, please."

"Yes, sir."

Her heartbeat jumped a little before she again slid to the other side of the car and belted herself in. *Why are we headed to his home? And why couldn't we stay longer at the gala? I'd looked forward to it, to the dancing and I admit, I wanted to show off the dress, which had clearly been the most beautiful gown there. Heck, I spent more time getting ready than we actually spent at the event.*

Roark sat across from her this time. He turned on

the lights. "I'm really sorry for the way this evening has turned out."

She looked out the window with feigned interest. "At least the children will still get their money, and that is the most important thing." Then she looked back at him. "Why did we leave? Are you embarrassed by me?"

"No! You could never embarrass me." He ran a hand through his hair. "I'm afraid I haven't explained myself very well."

She snorted a laugh. "Very well? You haven't explained yourself at all."

His mouth turned down at the corners. "That's true. I'm having George take us to my home. I want to change vehicles and I want to take you somewhere special."

Her pulse raced. "Somewhere special?"

He nodded. "Yes. You might have already been there before, but even if you have, it's still wonderful. You'll need a bit more coat, but I'll give you one of mine that will work for this trip."

With the lights in the limo's interior on, she could actually see the excitement on his face.

They arrived at Roark's home in Cherry Hills.

The enormous house was brick, with a circular driveway and covered entry. It looked like she was arriving at a really nice hotel.

"My parents also live here when they are in town. It's sort of a family home. This is where we celebrate the holidays, so it has to be large enough to accommodate everyone."

"So how large is large?" She looked up at the house, mansion really.

"Well, I have two brothers and their families, my parents and me, so we have nine bedrooms and ten bathrooms. There's an outdoor pool for use in the summer and an indoor pool for the winter. We also have a separate building holding the gym, with a hot tub and a sauna. If you want, I'll give you a tour when we get back. For now, though, I'd like to get coats and the convertible Camaro."

George opened the passenger door.

Roark exited the vehicle and held his hand out to help her. He turned to his driver. "George, I won't need you any longer. Have a good night."

"Yes, sir. Thank you."

The driver smiled and returned to the limo. He pulled away as she stared at the house.

The building was beautiful, without being ostentatious. She figured most of the house was toward the back. She couldn't see it.

Roark grabbed her hand and led her inside.

The entryway was huge, with marble flooring. On one side was a living room, with the dining room on the other.

He took her into the kitchen. Her entire loft would fit in it. She knew that was a bit of an exaggeration, but it was big. In the center was a horseshoe-shaped island with eight stools on one side and the sink, dishwasher, trash compactor, cupboards and drawers on the other.

They'd built in the refrigerator to look like part of the wall.

"Would you like a drink? On the other side of the kitchen is the bar. I have wine of several varieties, all from my vineyards, of course, and also beer and liquor for just about any mixed drink you desire."

Jessica laughed. "No, I'm fine. Why don't you go get your jackets?"

"Yes...the jackets. I almost forgot." He hurried out of the kitchen. "I'll be right back." He started out of the room.

"Roark. Is that you?" a woman called.

Roark hollered back. "Yes, Mom. It's me. Come meet someone."

His mother came around the wall into the kitchen. She was about Jessica's height and weight, with a beautiful figure. Her beautiful silver hair was cut into a stylish bob. It looked terrific on her. The style brought out her cheekbones.

"Hello. You must be Jessica. He hasn't been able to talk about anything or *anyone* since he met you."

Jessica felt her face heat and knew she blushed. "Is that right?"

Roark shrugged.

Marian clasped Jessica's hand. "Welcome to the family. I'll leave you two to do whatever you're doing."

Roark hugged his mother.

"I love you, son." Then she stepped back and left the kitchen.

Roark gathered Jessica into his arms and kissed her

on the forehead. "I need to get some jackets. I'll be right back"

Jessica touched her lips and smiled. How could he make her feel so alive when they'd only known each other for a matter of hours?

She looked around the kitchen and admired the light-colored granite of the kitchen countertops. This was a kitchen she could love. She loved to bake and would have lots of room for cooling the cookies. Her Monster Cookies made twenty dozen last time she made the whole recipe. She mixed the wet ingredients with her stand mixer and added that to the oatmeal, flour and other dry ingredients in a stockpot. Then had to mix them together with her hands, in rubber gloves, all in a stockpot.

Roark returned in a few minutes with two thick cable-knit sweaters. "You can put it over your head and keep your hair tucked in the neckline, so it doesn't blow with the top down."

"We're traveling with the top down?" Her voice went up a bit more than she'd meant. She hadn't figured on traveling with the top down. Joseph and Mandy had been in a convertible with the top down when they died. But she needed to remember that Joseph was a reckless driver, and that's why they died, not because of the car.

His eyebrows furrowed just a little, and he blinked a couple of times. "Yes, why else get the convertible?"

She shrugged. "Right, why?"

"Are you all right?"

She nodded. "I'm fine."

He frowned. "Are you sure? We don't have to do this."

"No, I want to see what you want to show me." And she realized she really did, because it was important to him and he wanted her to see it.

He smiled and pointed at the sweater she held. "Pull on your sweater now." He tugged the sweater over his head, mussing his perfect hair and making him look much more approachable.

She drew the garment over her head and did as he suggested and left her hair inside the sweater. The sleeves hung down almost to her knees. She chuckled.

"What's funny?"

"I feel like a kid in her daddy's sweater."

He smiled and shook his head as he came close. "Here, let's get these sleeves rolled up. I don't think pushing them will be enough."

She stretched out her arm. "Oh, I think it will. The sleeves have a good tight cuff. It will probably hold. If it doesn't then we'll roll them. So," she looked up at him. "Where are we going?"

Roark looked her up and down. "Are you Cinderella and have to be home before midnight?"

Deadpan, she answered. "Yes, but I turn into a pumpkin."

His eyes widened. "You're so serious. I'm not sure whether to believe you or not."

Suddenly, she burst out laughing. "You didn't seriously believe me?"

"No, but for a second, I wondered." Then he laughed. He came close and lifted her chin with a finger. "You're so beautiful. I've been dying to do this since I first saw you. May I kiss you?"

Her stomach turned somersaults. "I thought you'd never ask. Please do."

He lowered his head to her upraised face, angling and pressing his lips against hers.

The kiss was searing, and she felt it to her toes. Jessica tested his lips with her tongue and felt him smile as he opened enough for her to enter.

They tasted each other, circling, dueling, touching. Making love with their mouths.

Jessica pulled back, breathing hard, her pulse racing.

Roark lifted a thumb to her bottom lip and smoothed it over.

Her lips felt swollen from the most powerful kiss she'd ever had. "Wow!"

He smoothed his right knuckles over her jaw and then cupped it for just a moment.

She thought he was about to kiss her again.

Instead, he lowered his right hand to her waist. "Yes, wow, is a good way to describe a kiss like that. Shall we go before I figure a way to get you out of those clothes and into my bed?"

She lifted her chin as heat rose to points in her cheeks and she knew she blushed...because she could picture them in bed together. "I'm not that kind of girl, Roark. You should know that up front."

He held her by her waist. "I'm glad you're not. Let's go." He took them out the side door and into the garage.

She stopped just inside the door and whistled. "Holy cow!" This was one of the few times she wished she'd been more of a gear-head and could recognize all the kinds of cars. Her dad would have loved the six-car garage and every car in it. She knew for sure there was a silver Jaguar with the sleek cat hood ornament. It was the one with the fast back.

He walked over to the black convertible.

She followed, and from their earlier conversation, she knew it was a Camaro. And he had the candy-apple-red Mustang he drove yesterday. That was the extent of her car knowledge. Except he also had a dark blue pickup hooked up to a charger on the wall. That had to be a Ford Lightning. She'd seen the commercials at her mother's. The green car and the white car were makes she didn't know of. "You have a lot of vehicles."

He stood next to her on the passenger side of the Camaro. "I'm a bit of a car junkie. I have another garage in downtown Denver that is filled with cars, trucks and motorcycles. I'll take you over there one day."

She ran her hand lovingly over the black paint, which shone like it was covered in moonlight. "My dad would have loved to see them. He was a bit of a car junkie, too."

"We'll plan a meeting. Perhaps your mother and my

parents can meet for lunch and then we'll go to the garage."

"I can't speak for her, but I'll ask."

His brows formed slashes over his eyes, and he waved a hand in front of him. "No...no, of course not. I'm sorry. I don't mean to push so hard. I want us to get to know each other before our families get involved, as I'm sure you do, too."

She nodded. "That's exactly what I was thinking."

He opened the passenger door on the Camaro and held it until she was buckled in, then closed it. Then he walked around the car to the driver's side and climbed in.

He was so tall, the seat looked like he set it all the way back. Not that she minded. She liked the fact she could wear her three-and four-inch heels, and he'd still be taller.

"Ready?"

"Yup. All buckled up."

"Then let's do this. I can't wait for you to see it."

I can't either. Anything that gets him so excited, I want to see, to be part of. I wonder what it will be that is so incredible.

CHAPTER 5

*J*essica enjoyed the ride as Roark drove west toward the mountains.

He turned off I-70 at the exit for Lookout Mountain and headed towards Buffalo Bill's Grave and Museum. They reached the turnoff for the tourist attraction, but he drove past it. He started down the Lariat Trail, a road listed on the National Register of Historic Places and known for its seven hairpin turns in just five miles. Several turns later, he pulled to the side of the road.

"Look up. What do you see?"

"Stars?"

"Yes, stars. You can't see many in town because of all the light pollution, but you can see some here. I'll take you a little farther west and you'll be amazed. For now, look out east."

She did and saw the vista of Denver and the suburbs laid out before her in spectacular color from all the lights. "It's beautiful. The town looks so peaceful from up here."

He reached over and took her hand. "It does."

They looked a little longer, and he held her hand the whole time.

Then he turned around and went back the way they had come and headed west on I-70 again. This time, he stopped by the buffalo pens. Denver's lights were far enough away they couldn't be seen and so the stars absolutely carpeted the sky. The view was amazing.

Laying her head against the headrest, she looked up at a sky that took her back in time to one of her historical stories. The sky seemed magical. "When my dad and I would go camping, we'd see stars like this, carpeting the sky so that locating the planets was difficult. Dad had a small telescope, and we'd look through it to find them."

"That's a nice memory. Jessica, I know we haven't known each other for very long, but I believe there is something special between us. I'd like for you to accompany me to my ranch in Montana next week. There is a strong Wi-Fi signal so you can work there. I don't want to interfere with your livelihood."

She narrowed her eyes a little in thought. "I don't know. We really just met and don't know each other at all." *Regardless of this pull that I feel toward you. I like everything about you. She smiled to herself. Except when you ordered for me.*

He turned in the seat so his body was angled toward hers. "What better way to get to know one another than spending the week together? If you're worried about having sex, I won't even suggest it."

Should I spend the week with Roark? Do I trust him? I'm wildly attracted to him, more so than I've ever been with anyone else. So much so, I'd like to tear his clothes off right now. And didn't Lanie say to live life fully?

I'll do it. I'll go with him to Montana. After all, I'll only live once and I do want to get to know him better and if things don't work out, I'll stay in my bedroom and work. It will be excellent research for my book either way, though I'll make it a happily-ever-after ending.

She nodded, and half smiled. "That's right. I can. Very well, I'll come with you."

He smiled, and it reached his eyes, which crinkled with crow's feet. "Thank you. I know you'll enjoy it. Pack a swimsuit, and clothes for riding. Maybe even some for camping and fishing. If you want to dip your pole in the water, there is a great place to do it."

She clasped her hands in her lap. "It sounds like fun. My dad would have loved all of that." She heard the slight catch in her voice that was still there ten years after losing him.

He turned and took her left hand in his. Then he gave her a little squeeze. "I'm sorry he's not here to come with us. I would have loved to get to know him."

Liking the warmth of his hand around hers, she let her hand remain in his. "I'd have liked that, and I believe you would have liked each other."

He gave her hand a last squeeze and then started the car. He put the roof up, then crossed over the bridge and headed back to town. When he reached her building, he stopped next to the curb. He didn't move to get out.

Neither did she.

"Thank you for a wonderful evening."

She smiled and looked down before raising her gaze back to his. "I'm the one who should say that to you. This has been one of my most memorable dates ever."

He grinned and took her hand in his. "I'm glad to be memorable."

Jessica chuckled and shook her head. "Now, you're fishing for compliments, but I guess you deserve that one."

Roark grinned. "Already you know me so well. Just think how much better we'll know each other after our trip."

She lowered her chin. "That's true. I just hope we like what we find out. After all, we might not."

"I don't believe that for a minute, but we'll see. I guess I better get you inside." He got out of the car and went around to open her door.

She pulled his sweater over her head and left it on the seat before setting her feet on the ground.

He held out his hand.

She took it with a smile.

They walked hand-in-hand to the door.

She put in her code, and the door clicked. "You can leave me here. I'm quite safe now."

His eyebrows came together just enough to form

the small lines between them. "I wouldn't think of it. I'll walk you to your door."

She walked inside and down the hall to her loft. Her loft was in a nice, restored building downtown. It was nothing she was ashamed of, rather the opposite. She was very proud of her building and the way it sat back from the banks of the Platte River.

He went with her.

She unlocked her door. "Would you like to come in for a drink? I even have some of your wine."

"As much as I'd like that, you are *too* tempting right now." He pulled her close. "But I do want a goodnight kiss."

Jessica really couldn't believe that he was interested in someone like her. She wasn't sophisticated or rich. She made a decent living and had purchased her loft. But right now, none of that mattered. She wrapped her arms around his neck. "I'd like that ver—"

His lips made her forget whatever it was she was about to say.

She felt like he was making love to her with his mouth, and she returned the response as she tangled her fingers in his hair and held him close, not ready for the kiss to end. Never ready for the kiss to end. But if she let it go on, she'd be dragging him inside to make love. She backed away. Blood rushed in her ears as her heart pounded. Why was it like this from just a kiss with him?

He rubbed her bottom lip with the pad of a thumb. "I love kissing you."

"I love kissing you, too, but I need to stop. I have to stop." She already regretted the decision and wished she hadn't hit pause.

He kept his hands on her waist. "I understand and agree. I don't want us to go farther until we're ready to. I want it to be a conscious decision, not *just* a biological one."

"I agree, although biology looks pretty good right now."

He laughed. "It does, doesn't it?"

She lifted onto her toes and kissed his cheek. "Good night, Mr. Sullivan. I'll see you soon. What time will you pick me up and on Friday or Saturday?"

He took out his wallet. "I'll send you an email. Here's my card with my personal phone number and email. Send me one, so I'll have your email address."

She took the card. "All right. Have a good night."

"You, too, sweetheart."

Upon hearing the endearment, her pulse raced. *Sweetheart. Am I really his sweetheart?* She turned, entered the loft and closed the door after her, leaning against it for a bit. Then she took off her shoes, waltzed and twirled from the living room through the kitchen and into the bedroom, where she danced into the closet. She put her shoes on the shelf in their place. Then, with some difficulty, she unzipped her dress, stepped out of it and placed it on a hanger by the little hidden straps. She hung it with her other formal gowns. They looked cheap and tacky compared to her beautiful red gown. Lanie was right, and Jessica would donate them all to charity, most likely for Halloween costumes.

Tonight, because of the dress and because of Roark, she felt particularly attractive, so she put on her silk nightgown. It was the sexiest thing she'd owned until the dress Roark had gifted her. She ran her hands over her body. She loved the way the silk clung in all the right places. She'd take this one with her to Montana.

The next morning, Jessica woke up and got ready to go see her mother. On Sundays, they always had dinner together. Actually, it was a late lunch, but her mother always called it dinner because she was from Texas. Her father's family were farmers, and they also called the midday meal dinner and the evening meal supper.

She gathered up the dress, carefully folding it into the box it arrived in, to show it to her mother.

Jessica could have taken a picture, but a photo simply didn't capture all the nuances of the gown or the way it felt or moved. She also wanted to tell her she was going to Montana with Roark. That bit of news would probably not go over well, but there was something between her and Roark that she couldn't explain, and wanted to explore. Why did she desire this man more than she had any man she'd known? Why did she want him even more than she had Joseph, her fiancé? She needed her mother's opinion on what Jessica felt when she was with him.

Her mother was in the kitchen already cooking when Jessica arrived at her home. Based on the wonderful smells wafting under her nose, they were having a pork roast for dinner. It was one of Jessica's favorite meals because she never cooked one for herself. And she knew her mother always made her famous mashed potatoes and gravy, Jessica's favorite things to eat and something she could never get right. She could make the potatoes, but no matter how many times she watched her mother, she could never make the gravy. It either clumped or tasted like flour or was too thin or too thick, never perfect like her mother's.

Of course, she had to watch how much she ate because she didn't want to gain any weight. The dress fit perfectly right now. She wanted to wear it again and that meant not even one extra pound. She wasn't one who dieted, but she watched what she ate. She was of the opinion that no food was forbidden.

She walked over to her mother, who stood at the stove stirring what looked like the gravy. She hugged her from behind. "Hi, Mom."

"Hi, Jessie. Set the table, would you, please?"

"Sure."

"Set it for three. Mr. Brandt is coming over for dinner."

Jessica raised her eyebrows. "Mr. Brandt. You mean Uncle Philip? Dad's best friend?"

"He called on me a couple of weeks ago, and we've been having some wonderful conversations. We've gone out to dinner twice, and I invited him to dinner today. I want your opinion. I value it, but I'm also happier than I've been since your father died. Philip and I have a lot of things in common and not just that our spouses have died. It's becoming serious, and I wanted you to know."

"Mom, I'm thrilled for both of you. I know he's been as unhappy since Aunt Jean passed as you have been since losing Dad. It's time for you both to find some happiness again. That it's together is wonderful. You've known each other for years already, so there's no awkward silences." She hugged her mother again. "I have some news myself. That matchmaker you sent me to, Mrs. Madison, at Love International, set me up with someone."

"I know, a Mr. Sullivan, if I remember correctly."

"Yes, *Roark Sullivan* of Sullivan International Holding Co. He and I signed up the same day and were matched." The more she talked about and thought about Roark, the better she felt about going to Montana. Her stomach was filled with butterflies. "Oh, Mom. He's wonderful. I've never felt like this about anyone, not even Joseph. Maybe that's why he cheated with Mandy. Maybe he found something with her he couldn't find with me."

Her mother should be happy. She still had a long life ahead of her, and she should have companionship and, hopefully, even love.

"Mom, I'm going with Roark to his ranch next week."

"Oh, that will be nice. You love to ride horses and all of that stuff you and your father used to do."

Jessica's jaw dropped. That was not the response she was expecting from her mother. She pulled the plates out of the cupboard on the right side of the sink and glasses from the cupboard to the left side next to the refrigerator.

She set the plates and glasses on the dining room table and then retrieved the silverware. "Yes, I do. But I want you to know that…well…his ranch is in Montana. We'll fly to Bozeman on his private jet on Friday and probably return on Thursday or Friday of the following week. I'll be taking my laptop with me so I can work if the weather turns bad."

Her mother lifted an eyebrow and looked at Jessica. "You're a grown woman. Twenty-seven years old now, and you don't need your mother's permission to do anything. I'm glad you feel comfortable enough to tell me what you're doing. I like that you trust in our relationship enough to do that."

She hugged her mother. "Of course. You're my best friend and my mother. I always take your opinions into consideration. I might not agree, but I do consider them." She looked at the gravy on the stove and pointed at it. "You need to stir the gravy."

"Oh, my goodness." Sally turned off the burner, then used the skirt of her apron to pick up the pan and take it to the sink. "I'm afraid I ruined it."

"You still have drippings. Just make some more. If Uncle Philip comes, I'll take care of the gravy while you see to him."

Her mother put together the sauce and stirred it.

The doorbell rang.

"Let me go get him."

Sally chuckled. "All right. Go. He won't believe how much you've changed. You're not that teenaged girl he knew from your daddy's funeral ten years ago."

Jessica hurried to the door and opened it. Standing on the stoop was a man about her height with beautiful silver hair and a floral bouquet.

"Oh, Uncle Philip, you didn't need to get me flowers."

He laughed. "Give us a hug, you cheeky girl. These are for your mother." He opened his arms wide.

Jessica went into them and hugged him tight. She received a bear hug in return. "Come on inside. I'll take those and put them in some water. Mom's cooking." She turned and headed toward the kitchen.

Philip followed.

They entered the kitchen and her mother turned and beamed at Philip.

"Sally. You look beautiful, as always." He gave her a peck on the cheek.

"Oh, Philip." Her mother waved away the compliment.

Jessica felt like the third wheel. She would stay for dinner, but then she'd leave. Lanie would suddenly have a crisis or something. Besides, she needed to talk to Lanie and tell her how the date went. Jessica smiled at who could soon become her parents. "Mom, the gravy."

Sally startled. "Oh, my." She turned toward the stove and stirred the contents of a saucepan. "Thank you, dear. It wouldn't have been good to ruin two batches of gravy."

"I should say not." Jessica put her hands on her hips. "What would I put on my potatoes?" Then she chuckled. "I'll get the food on the table. I believe the salad, peas and potatoes are done. The crescent rolls are ready to come out of the oven. Perhaps Uncle Philip would carve the roast for us?"

"Of course, I'd be happy to."

"The roast has been resting. It's under that aluminum foil on the counter." Her mother pointed to the tented meat.

Jessica placed the dishes of food on the table, except for the pork.

In a few minutes, Sally and Philip emerged from the kitchen and Jessica would have sworn her mother looked like she'd been thoroughly kissed. Her hair was a little mussed, and she blushed like a schoolgirl.

Philip was no better. He set the roast on the table and then ran a hand through his hair.

It didn't help, and Jessica had to work hard not to laugh. But soon all the food was served, and any thought of laughing or talking fled her mind and was filled instead with dinner. It was wonderful. Her mother was still the best cook. She wished she'd inherited some of that knowledge. Alas, she wasn't a cook. She was a baker, though, and should have brought her chocolate layer cake, but she didn't have a chance to bake it yesterday.

After dinner, the three of them retired to the living room.

"Mom, I need to go, but I wanted you to see the dress Roark gave me. It's the most beautiful thing I own." She went to the coat closet and retrieved the gown. Still struck by its beauty, she held it up for her mother to see in its full glory. "Well, what do you think? It fits like a glove...like it was made just for me."

Phillip and Sally sat on the sofa. "Who is Roark?"

"Roark Sullivan of Sullivan International Holdings, Inc.," Jessica explained.

"Well, well. That is some interesting news." Philip turned to Sally. "Why didn't you tell me?"

Sally shrugged. "I didn't really know anything, and now you know as much as I do." She reached out and felt the dress. "It's beautiful. Are those real gems?"

"I don't know." Jessica examined the stones again. "They look like it, don't they? But surely, even Roark wouldn't have real gemstones on a dress...would he?"

Sally smiled as she touched the dress. "Where did the dress come from?"

"Veronica Sattler's House of Design."

Sally's eyes widened, and she yanked her hand away. "Really? Well, considering some of her other creations, they could very well be real. You know, Veronica's built a lot like we are, and they always make very long the dresses so they can sew the hem for the individual client. She might have made this for herself and she could very well have put real gemstones on it."

Jessica looked at the dress again, but with new appreciation. "Oh, my God. I should put this in my safe deposit box." She looked over at her mother. "I need a bigger box."

Sally and Philip laughed.

Philip pointed at the dress. "Just keep it in your closet and don't cover it with plastic. I read it does something bad to the material during long-term storage. You're better off using a pillowcase with the bottom seam opened just enough for the hanger to slip through. Or you could just keep it in the box it came in."

"I don't want the folds to make permanent wrinkles in the material, so no to keeping it in the box." Jessica cocked a brow. "How do you know this stuff?"

Philip grinned and cocked a brow, mimicking her. "I read all kinds of things,k and that was one bit of housekeeping hints I read."

"Well, it makes sense to me and I will definitely do the pillow case tonight."

Jessica was happy to see her mother so content with Philip. They were clearly in love. Would she and Roark look like that someday? Did they already look like that? No, it was too soon to even think about love, but that is the first thing that popped into her mind when she thought about him.

She gave her mother a kiss and a hug. "I need to go, Mom. I'll see you in a couple of weeks."

"Have fun on your vacation."

"I will." Jessica looked into the living room. "Goodbye, Uncle Philip. It was good to see you."

Philip stood and walked over to her. "Have a good time. I enjoyed seeing you. Perhaps we'll see more of each other now."

"Oh, I'm sure we will." She gave him a kiss on the cheek. "Be good to Mom or I'll have to kill you." She laughed.

He grinned. "If I treat her less than well, you have my permission to do just that. Now go. Have fun."

As she was leaving, she glanced back and saw her mother and Philip standing next to each other. He had his arm around Sally's shoulders. She wondered when the wedding bells would be tolling.

Heading home, she thought about her own relationship with Roark. Two days! It had only been two days, and she felt like she'd known him forever.

What would their trip to Montana bring?

CHAPTER 6

*J*essica was ready when Roark knocked on the door Friday morning. She had two large suitcases. In one, were her waders, fly rod and reel, and her fishing vest with all her flies. She'd had it all packed away in storage since her father passed. She hadn't been sure if she would ever get to use them again. The thought of using them again pleased her very much. It was almost like bringing her dad back for a little while.

She answered the door, and Roark looked good enough to eat. He wore a pair of well-worn jeans that fit very nicely. Along with the jeans, he wore a long-sleeved Henley shirt with the sleeves pushed up to the elbow, emphasizing his muscular forearms.

"Hi. Come on in."

He did.

She closed the door behind him. When she turned

around, he hadn't moved, and she nearly ran into him. "Oh."

"Sorry." He wrapped his arms around her. "But not really. I've wanted you in my arms all week, but I did my best to stay away."

"You did very well. I haven't seen you."

"Did you miss me?"

She lifted her chin. "I don't know you well enough to miss you."

He smiled. "Ah, but I bet you thought about me."

"So what? I thought about you. I told my mother about you."

"That's a good thing." He leaned down and kissed her softly.

It was more of a peck than a proper kiss, and Jessica wanted more. She snaked her hand around his neck and into his hair, pulling his head down. Then she kissed him. *Really* kissed him, with all the feelings that roared inside her. She *had* missed him. How was that possible? She finally pulled back and stepped out of his arms.

She lifted a brow. "Now, *that* was a kiss."

His eyebrows rose in a slow arch. "Yes, ma'am. I do believe that's one of the best kisses I've ever had. And that's saying a lot."

His words gave her a brief twinge of insecurity because he was so much more experienced than she was.

"But we need to get going. Are these your suitcases?"

"Yes."

He lifted his brows. "Two? For a week's stay?"

"Well, I just never know when I'll fall in the river and need clean dry clothes, plus I brought my chest waders, fly rod and reel."

"You really are the outdoors woman."

"It's true. I love the outdoors, and spending time in the sunshine is good for you. Vitamin D and all that."

"I enjoy being outside when I'm on the ranch, not so much when I'm in town."

"I agree. Would you get one of my suitcases, please?"

"Of course, I'll take them both. You can bring your laptop and handbag, if you have one."

"Have you ever met a woman who didn't carry a purse?" She laughed as she picked up her computer bag and her purse.

He grabbed the handles of both her suitcases and lifted them rather than rolling them. "Actually, no, I haven't."

Jessica locked her loft door and followed Roark out of the building to the limo.

George hurried to take the bags from Roark and put them in the trunk. Then he returned. "Would you like that in the trunk, too, Miss Kirby?" He pointed at her computer bag.

"Yes, thank you, George." She handed him the bag and then got in the car, sitting on the backseat.

Roark followed and sat next to her this time. He took her hand and held it while they rode to the airport.

His plane was at the Rocky Mountain Metropolitan Airport in Broomfield. The drive was easy because they were traveling against the flow of rush hour traffic.

When they arrived, George pulled up next to the door of a hangar.

"You have a hangar for you plane?" She saw several other hangars, but none were as large as this one. Small single and double engine planes, most with propellers, were all over the asphalt in front of the hanger, but far enough away that she thought he could still get out.

"Yes, it just makes sense to me. I avoid damage from the elements." He pointed at the little planes. "Especially sun and wind, therefore I don't have to have it repainted as often and I don't have rust problems either. Upkeep and maintenance are easier for my employees to perform as well."

"That makes sense."

"That's what people don't understand about having a jet. It's more than just the cost of the plane and fuel. It's upkeep, tune-ups, painting and anything else that needs to be done. My employees to do those tasks find it easier if they aren't fighting the elements, too."

She nodded. "I get that."

George opened the door and held his hand out. "Miss Kirby."

She took his hand. "Thank you, George."

"My pleasure, miss."

Roark exited the car, walked with her to the door to the hangar, and opened it for her to enter.

Seeing the jet was almost more than she could imagine. Luckily, her imagination was highly active, and she couldn't wait to see the inside.

"Oh, my, this is amazing."

Roark took her hand and led her to the plane. "Come on. Let's get settled." He released her hand at the bottom of the stairs.

She ascended the rolling staircase and entered what looked like a living room with two sofas on one wall. Opposite them was a large-screen television with a recliner on each of the lower corners.

"Come with me. I'll show you the plane." Roark took her hand again. "As you can see, this is the living room. The next one is the dining room."

They entered the room, and she saw a beautiful black lacquered table with eight black high-backed chairs. The back of each chair was padded up the middle with the same silver-gray material that covered the seat. The back had a one-inch gold strip blocking the padding. Another television hung on the wall shared with the living room, which was opposite the head of the table.

Next up was the kitchen. One side sported a sink, a full-sized refrigerator, and a four-burner stove with counter space between each appliance. Across from them was a wine cooler and cupboards and more counters. All the counter space was a beautiful black granite with gold lines streaking through it.

Leaving the kitchen, she entered a private sitting area with another large-screen television and a semicircle sofa she could lie on if she wanted to. A large desk was on the wall opposite the entryway.

Next came the bedroom. She saw a queen-sized bed with a nightstand on either side, with a dresser and chest of drawers on the opposite wall.

Last was an enormous bathroom with double showers, a double sink, and separate closets with the dual commodes.

Roark led her back to the living room and settled them on one of the couches. "What do you think?"

She let out a deep breath. "I'm overwhelmed. I've never seen anything like this. Or been on any plane like this. I could live here quite happily, just parked in a field somewhere."

He chuckled. "I'll build you a house like this in that field somewhere."

She withdrew her hand from his and stood, then paced. "I don't think you understand. This is all so much. I don't know how to process it. I like you very much, but I don't want this to be about your money. I don't want to get caught up in that spiderweb where I feel obligated just because of the money. Can you understand?"

He stood and went to her, taking her in his arms.

She laid her head on his chest.

"Sweetheart, I don't want it to be about the money, either. I can imagine it's hard for you to accept, but I hope that you'll just try to see me as just a man. See how it goes this week, and then we'll discuss this more. Give me that chance."

She looked up and leaned back, sure he wouldn't let her go. "All right. I want this week to be about fun. I haven't been to a ranch or riding or camping for a very long time. Not since my dad died ten years ago."

"That's a long time. I hope I can give you as wonderful memories as he gave you. You deserve it."

"Thanks."

The speaker sounded overhead. "Please prepare for takeoff. We'll be taxiing out to the runway for a couple of minutes, and then we'll be in the air. Flying time is approximately one hour and forty minutes. We should be at the hangar in Bozeman about ten minutes after landing."

She looked around her for a seatbelt. "Where do we sit to buckle up?"

He released her and pointed at all the chairs and sofas. "Anywhere you want. Though I recommend the chairs for takeoffs and landings. They feel sturdier, if you know what I mean. I think because there are two arms, not just one, as on the end of the sofa."

She picked a chair with a small table between it and the next chair.

Roark sat in the chair beside hers.

Five minutes later, they were in the air.

"You may walk about the cabin now. They forecast the weather to be clear all the way to Bozeman." The microphone clicked off.

Roark unbuckled his seatbelt and stood. "Would you like something to drink? We have just about every-thing from water to bourbon."

"It's a little early for alcohol, so how about coffee? I didn't have mine this morning and could really use some, or I'll be falling asleep on one of those couches."

"Coffee coming up." Roark headed toward the kitchen.

Jessica followed. She leaned against a counter, out of his way. "Do you usually take care of yourself when you fly, or do you have an employee who normally serves you on board?"

He took the single-cup coffee maker out of a cupboard under the counter next to the stove. Then he filled it with water and plugged it into the wall socket. "I do for myself, most of the time. When I have a lot of guests, I have a couple of flight attendants who look after us. Rob and Laura Gentry are a married couple who used to be flight attendants for United Airlines. When they retired, they came to work for me. They've been with me for about five years now."

When the coffeemaker was ready, he opened a drawer filled with coffee pods. "What kind would you like?"

She walked over and stared into the drawer. "Anything with double caffeine."

"I've got just the thing. I like it when I have a lot of meetings scheduled." He popped the pod into the machine, closed it and pressed Start.

As the scent of freshly brewed coffee hit her nostrils, Jessica closed her eyes. "Mmm. There's nothing like the smell of fresh coffee. It revs up all my senses and gets me ready for the day."

He came up behind her and put his arms around her waist. "I know something else that can rev up your senses for the day."

She laughed and then took a sip of the coffee. "Mmm. This is so good. And no, you don't. Men cannot rev me up like my first cup of coffee in the morning."

He kissed her neck behind her ear.

She shivered and couldn't pretend that she hadn't felt anything.

"Are you sure about that?" He kissed her again, this time on the other side of her neck.

The kiss nearly made her knees weak. "Yes, I'm sure. But you can continue to try."

He chuckled and turned her in his arms.

She set her coffee on the counter.

"You're a liar, Miss Kirby." He lowered his head and placed a line of fiery kisses down her throat.

I'm so glad I wore a tank top today. "Am I? You can continue to try to change my mind."

He gently nipped her neck, licked it, and followed that with a kiss. "How about now?"

Her knees buckled.

He didn't let her fall.

She wrapped her arms around his neck. "You are a wicked, wicked man, Mr. Sullivan."

"I am, Miss Kirby, and I don't know how I'll manage to keep from taking you to bed for the next hour and a half, but I will prevail...for you."

Jessica had never felt more cared for or more turned on in her life, but she wouldn't act on it. She wasn't interested in jumping into the sack for one night and perhaps losing a lifetime of love. And she felt that was where this could go. Maybe. If she could get over him being so wealthy.

"You're thinking. What are you thinking about?" He didn't release her, but the kisses stopped and a wrinkle bridged the expanse of his forehead.

"I was thinking about us...down the road...and what I want from this relationship. First, I guess I need to figure out if we have a relationship at all."

His gaze slipped to hers as he held her close. "Jessica, my darling, we have a relationship, or at least a good start on one. Neither of us has ever been knocked over by a kiss before like we were that first time, and for me at least, every time since then."

She lowered her gaze to his chest for a moment and then looked up. "Me, too. I've never felt like that." She brought a hand away from his neck and motioned between them. "Like this. But I don't want to ruin it by moving too fast. I want to make sure it's the real thing."

"So do I. So, what would you like to do? After I get a cup of coffee." He set up the machine again.

"Do you have cards on board, and do you play poker?" She sucked in her lower lip before grinning.

He lowered his eyelids to half-staff and cocked an eyebrow. "I might. What are the stakes?"

"Well, I'd say strip poker, but that's not taking it slow and I don't want the first time I see you naked to be because of a game."

"I agree. I want to undress you slowly and kiss every inch of skin that I reveal."

She let out a breath and fanned herself. "Whoa. Did it suddenly get hot in here?"

He laughed.

So did she. "Do you have matchsticks or a lot of change?"

He opened a couple of drawers under the counter across from the stove and pulled out a box of kitchen matches. "Here we go. We use them for the candles in the bedroom. How many do you want?"

"Let's say fifty each. That way there are enough sticks left, we can make withdrawals—because you will definitely need to. I'm going to beat the pants off you, so to speak."

He laughed and dug the cards out of another drawer and grabbed his coffee. Then they went to the dining room and played.

The time went by so fast; it startled her when the captain's voice sounded. "We are starting our final descent into Bozeman. Please return to your seats and fasten your seatbelts."

He gathered the matches and placed them in the box. "You weren't kidding about your expertise with poker. You should have nearly two hundred matches, since I had to get into the bank twice."

She laughed as she gathered the cards and put them back in the pack. "Maybe I should have played strip poker, after all. Who knew you were such a terrible player?"

His mouth formed a flat line. "I'm better when I'm playing for something that matters. Matchsticks don't."

"Yeah, I suppose that's true."

When everything was set to rights and returned to its home for landing, Jessica and Roark went back to the living area. This time they sat together on the sofa, buckled up, and then Roark took her hand. He seemed to enjoy touching her—almost as if he needed it.

Jessica's stomach turned over, and it had nothing to do with the plane's descent. It had everything to do with her trepidation about this week. What if things went wrong and she and Roark discovered they were too different? So many other questions ran through her mind, each one landing with a thud in her stomach. She had to stop this and trust that they would like each other. *Please let us continue to like each other.*

CHAPTER 7

*I*t surprised Jessica to see a dark blue Chevy Yukon waiting at the airport. Its driver was a tall, lanky cowboy dressed in jeans, a plaid shirt, and a black cowboy hat that had definitely seen better days. It was probably perfect for the work he did. Hats worn every day needed to be comfortable, and his obviously was.

"Good to see you, Seth. I expected your dad. Is Mannie tied up with the cows?"

"Yeah, several of the cows decided to have trouble giving birth, so he's been out with a few of the boys, pulling calves. Didn't figure you'd mind being picked up by me."

"No, that's just fine." Roark turned to Jessica. "This is my friend, Jessica Kirby. She'll be here with me this week."

Seth tipped his hat. "Pleased to meet you, Miss Kirby."

She held out her hand. "Pleased to meet you, too, Seth."

He accepted her hand and shook it.

The captain and first mate came over to them with their bags.

Captain Ralston set the bags down next to the SUV. "Mr. Sullivan, are you still planning on going home next Friday?"

"That is the plan. Please get the plane ready for that date."

"Yes, sir. Have a pleasant week."

"We intend to. Thank you, Captain Ralston." He placed his hand on the back of Jessica's waist and guided her to the Yukon.

He opened the back passenger door of the SUV.

Jessica entered, sat, and buckled up.

Roark closed the door and walked around to the other side where he got in and buckled up, too.

After loading the luggage, Seth closed the rear hatch and got behind the wheel. "Everyone buckled? The road gets rough in places, Miss Kirby, and you'll be glad you've got your seatbelt on."

"Thank you for your concern, Seth."

"Yes, miss." Seth pulled the vehicle out of the airport and onto the highway.

They'd been driving for around twenty minutes when Seth turned off onto a two-lane road.

The landscape along the highway was mostly empty grassland. There a few cows in one fenced pasture and horses in another. After they turned onto a two-lane road, the land on either side became more what she considered as ranch land. Pastures with lots of cattle and horses. She even saw one with sheep. She'd set a couple of books in Montana, but never with shepherds.

Roark pointed and made a complete circle with his arm. "You've been on my land for about the last fifteen minutes. Another five will put us in the driveway to the house."

"That's incredible. Will we be able to ride today?

He took her hand and squeezed it. "We'll be able to ride to your heart's content.

She grinned. Her body felt like it had released all her adrenalin, and she was more excited the closer they got to the ranch. "I can hardly wait."

"Sure. I know just the horse for you. She's a pretty little black mare with a soft mouth and easy manner. You'll like her. We call her Sunny, for her disposition."

"She sounds perfect." Her stomach leaped at the thought of being in the saddle again. "Does she still have some spirit? Will she be able to keep up with you?"

"Oh, yes. I'll ride her son. He's also a black like Sunny. He's her first colt and is about four-years-old now. She's about eight, but still thinks she's a filly." He chuckled. "I guarantee you'll like her, but if you don't, we have plenty of others you can choose from."

"She sounds wonderful. I'd like to get settled in my room and get my boots on before we go riding."

"That's fine. I want you to meet my cook and head

housekeeper, Athena Mack. Her husband Jubal is my head wrangler. Both of them have been with me since the beginning, over fifteen years now." He rubbed his fingers over his chin like he was stroking a goatee. "I can't believe it's been that long. Athena and Jubal have practically run this spread by themselves for years. I just pay the bills. They've done the hiring, along with my foreman, Mannie Frederick. Seth is his son."

"Did you buy the ranch this big, or have you expanded?"

"It was about a quarter this size when I bought it. Since then, I've purchased the surrounding ranches as they were inherited. If the kids wanted to sell, for whatever reason, I'd buy them. It's hard for the smaller spreads to make a living and pay the ranch bills. Some people are tired of working so hard for nothing. Most of them have sold to me and then come to work for me, doing the same thing they used to but without all the bills and a paycheck instead."

"It's nice they can still do what they love."

"It is, and if they want to stay living where they are, they can, or I have new homes for the families here."

"This is quite the operation."

"It takes many people. People who put money back into the local economy. It's a win-win for everyone, but probably mostly for me because I get the knowledge-able staff I need. I don't have to train them or worry about turnover."

"Here we are, folks. Home sweet home." Seth pulled

the SUV to a stop in front of a large two-story wooden home.

What looked like river rock decorated the bottom half of the first floor. Large stones that looked to be about four to six inches in diameter. A wide porch, with logs for the railings and the roof braces, looked like it ran all the way around the house, but she wasn't sure.

She was pleased to see a swing and a couple of rocking chairs on one side of the double doors, and a small table and four chairs on the other side. The arrangement was exactly how she would have done it.

They exited the car and stood next to it for a minute.

She gazed up at the house.

"Your home is beautiful, and I love the porch set up. Can you see the sunset from there?" She pointed to the swing.

Roark smiled. "You can, and I hope to show you tonight. We have some beautiful sunsets."

"I don't know. The sunsets looking over the mountains from my loft in Denver are hard to beat."

"Trust me. You'll enjoy this one. Shall we go inside?"

She gestured toward the back of the SUV. "What about the luggage?"

He turned back. "Seth, will you take Miss Kirby's bags up to the guest room, please?"

Seth already had the hatch open and was taking the suitcases out. "Sure will, Mr. Sullivan. You might want to take Miss Kirby to the barn. We've got a couple of new foals, one filly and one colt. They were both born about a week ago. They are the cutest little things."

Jessica turned to Roark. Her body was alive with longing. "Can we go now? I'd love to see them. I love babies."

He laughed. "Sure. It's this way." He put out his arm.

She placed her left hand through the crook of his elbow and covered it with her right hand. Jessica was happier than she'd been in a while and she knew a significant part of that was because of the man at her side.

They reached the enormous barn a few minutes later. Inside was bright with lots of overhead lights.

She counted twenty stalls on each side of the structure. The barn was two stories on the long sides and three stories in the center to accommodate the hay loft. Straw crunched under her feet where it had fallen when they mucked the stalls. The building smelled of horses, cows, straw, hay, and manure. Barn smells that she'd missed for so long.

Roark walked them down to the seventeenth stall on the right side. It and the next two were larger than the others. "These are our birthing stalls. This is the first time we've actually used two at once."

Inside the stall was a beautiful chestnut mare and a little black foal. As soon as they put their arms on the metal gate, he ducked behind his mama.

She jutted her chin toward the baby. "Is this the colt?"

"Let me see." He walked over to the post between

the seventeenth and eighteenth stalls and read from the small clipboard. "Yes, he's the colt. His mama is Bonnie Blue. I haven't named him yet. Would you like to name these two new ones?"

She looked up, her eyebrows high and her eyes wide. "Really?"

He laughed. "Yes, really. You're a writer and name characters all the time. I figure you'll give him a good name."

Jessica looked hard at the colt. Her eyes narrowed. She thought about how she would name her character. She'd named many horses in her books. "I think you should call him Blue Boy after his mother."

"I like that. Blue Boy, it is. Shall we look at the filly? I hate naming them, so you're saving me the trouble."

"Yes, I want to see her. I wish we could go in. I'd love to make friends with the mama's and their babies."

"The next mare is June Bug. She's the gentlest mare I have. Come on inside, she'll let you pet her and maybe her little filly will come over to you, too." He opened the gate and then closed it behind them.

Jessica walked slowly over to June Bug. "Hello, girl. How are you today? Will you let me pet you?" She reached out and petted her neck, then scratched her ears and down the front of her head. "You are such a pretty girl. Yes, you are. Do you think your baby will let me touch her?" She continued the ministrations and petting her neck. Then she wrapped her arms around the horse's neck and hugged her.

She felt a little push on her hip and looked down. The baby was nudging her with her nose.

Jessica chuckled and slowly got to her knees in front of the little buckskin filly. She didn't look anything like her mama, so Jessica figured she must take after her sire. She reached over, gently petted her neck and worked her way up to her ears and forelock. Then she smoothed her hand down the baby's muzzle and back up to scratch her ears. "You are so soft, so special." She whispered so as not to frighten the baby.

After a bit, the filly backed away, found her mother and began to nurse.

She stood and walked over to Roark. "She's beautiful. They both are."

He bent his knees to look at her straight in the face. "Are those tears I see in your eyes?"

"Yes, but you aren't supposed to notice. I get a little choked up when I see babies of any kind."

"I'll have to remember that and not take you to see James. He's my youngest brother, and he has twin sons who are just three months old."

"Oh, I would love to meet your brother and his family."

Roark laughed. "You just want to hold a baby. I know you. You just can't resist."

She smiled and turned to watch the young filly.

Roark put his arm around her shoulders and gave her a little squeeze. "If you still want to ride today, we need to get going."

"I do. Let's go back to the house so I can get on the

appropriate clothes." She looked back at the mama and filly before she practically ran back to the house.

Roark only had to walk a little faster to keep up with her because his strides were so long. He opened one of the front double doors. Twelve small window pane like features carved into each door. When she got close, she saw the scroll work that surrounded each of the little doors. They were beautiful and opened into a foyer. The stair case was directly in front of them. The living room was to the left.

Two sofas, facing each other over a rectangular coffee table, were upholstered with beige suede. They both had massive cushions on the seat and back. She was afraid she'd sink into the sofa and never be able to get up from it. Large brown leather recliners, one on either end of a sofa, faced the biggest TV screen she'd ever seen. She bet it was ninety inches. It would be like being in a theater. Of course, the recliners were facing the TV.

All that was besides the conversation pit. An indoor fire pit with three two-by-fours forming a counter for drinks and food surrounding it was in the center of the sunken living room. The pit was square with three over stuffed seats along each side.

"Do you like football?" She pointed at the screen.

"I better. I own a team."

Jessica's eyes widened, and she felt herself blush. "Oh, I guess you do like it. Otherwise, why own a team?"

"Because they are money makers. With the exceptions of the charities I support, I don't do anything that doesn't make money."

"Interesting." *Is making money all he's interested in?*

"Honey." He took her by the shoulders and turned her so she looked at him. "I wouldn't be where I am if I had companies that didn't make money. My shareholders wouldn't be happy and wouldn't support new ventures."

She looked into his emerald eyes. "I understand. I guess I don't think that way."

"Don't you? You write books. Would you keep writing, if your books didn't make money? You have a way to make a living, but if your books aren't doing that for you, you would have to quit, right?"

"You're right. I couldn't afford to keep writing for a living."

"Exactly my point. Let's go upstairs and we can both change clothes. Then you can meet Sunny and we'll take a ride. There's a pretty little place I'd like to show you."

She grinned and ran for the stairs directly in front of her, just outside the living room.

Roark caught up to her halfway up the stairs. "You'll get lost if you don't wait."

She continued up the stairs. "I thought I'd wait at the top of the stairs."

"You need more of a head start than that if you want to beat me."

"I'll remember that."

From the top of the stairs, he walked to the end of

the hall. "My room is here on the right. Yours is across the hall. I hope you find it comfortable."

"I'm sure it will be fine." She walked over to the door and entered. She stopped just inside after she shut the door. She looked around and realized this was the sitting room. Two doors led off into the sitting room. She opened one and found the bathroom. Marble double sinks with beautiful chrome faucets. *The other door must lead to the bedroom.*

As she walked farther into the sitting room, her jaw dropped lower and lower until she was afraid she'd step on it.

The sitting room was gigantic and decorated with rose wallpaper and rose brocade furniture. Her computer bag sat on the desk. Her suitcases were nowhere to be seen, so she assumed they were in the bedroom.

She headed there, into another breathtaking scene. Dominated by a king-size four-poster bed, the room still seemed big. Beside a bureau with a mirror stood a chest of drawers that was nearly as tall as she was. Beautifully carved nightstands sat on each side of the bed. The wood, either oak or maple, lent a warm feeling to the room, and all the furniture was made of the same wood.

Her suitcases were at the foot of the bed. She rolled them around to the side nearest the bureau and then lifted them onto the covers. She opened both and pulled out the clothes she needed. Shedding her outfit, she donned jeans, a soft, worn flannel shirt in a red plaid design, and her old, well-loved cowboy boots. Wishing she had a hat; she tied her long hair back into a ponytail.

She applied lip balm and was out the door.

Roark waited the hall. "You're faster than I thought you'd be."

"I knew exactly what I was going to wear." She looked at him and laughed. "I didn't know we were going as twins."

He, too, wore a red plaid flannel shirt with the sleeves rolled up. "Should I go change?"

"No. It doesn't bother me if it doesn't bother you."

"It doesn't. Let's head back out to the barn and introduce you to Sunny."

A smile spread across her face and she shoved her hands in her pockets to keep from doing a fist pump. "I can't wait." *I hope I remember how to ride. I don't want to embarrass myself by falling off in front of Roark.*

CHAPTER 8

Sunny was a pretty black mare. She came right up to Jessica and nudged her with her nose.

Jessica laughed. "Oh, you want to be petted and scratched, do you?" She petted her neck first and then scratched her ears and forelock. She rubbed her hand over the horse's nose, amazed at how soft it was. Not as soft as the new baby filly's was, but still very soft...like velvet. "Roark, I'll never get her saddled if she won't let me go."

"I'll saddle her. You just keep her still."

"I don't think that will be a problem." She reached up and placed her arms around the horse's neck as far as she could. "Will it, Sunny? No, that won't be a problem at all." She hugged her and kissed her neck, then moved in front of the horse and petted her from the forelock down her muzzle to her nose.

Roark finished saddling her in a few minutes.

"Done. Come meet her son. His name is Apollo, the Greek god of the sun."

They walked across the wide middle aisle toward the back of the barn and the twenty-first stall. Inside stood a magnificent coal-black stallion. His head was high and, as Roark approached, he came to the gate and waited.

Roark had grabbed a cookie from a bag on the post between stalls fifteen and sixteen. He came to the gate and first petted the horse before giving him the cookie. "That's a good boy. Are you ready to go for a ride?"

The horse shook his head up and down.

Her mouth opened wide and her hands went to her hips before she realized what she was doing. She closed her mouth. "Did he just answer you?"

"You saw it." He turned to the horse. "Did you just answer me?"

The horse nodded again.

Jessica laughed.

So did Roark. "He can answer yes and no to the questions we've taught him, but that's all. We haven't taught him to count or anything like that."

"I bet he could learn. He seems to be very smart."

Apollo nodded.

Jessica laughed again. The horse was entertaining, even if he didn't mean to be. "Why don't you get him saddled and let's ride?"

"It will only take a few minutes." When he finished, he took the reins. "Let's walk them outside."

She took her reins near Sunny's mouth and walked

her out of the barn. Outside, while Roark closed the doors, she mounted. It felt so good to be in the saddle again. She'd forgotten how much she liked horseback riding.

He mounted Apollo and led her around the barn in the direction of the gate into the pasture, where he dismounted and opened it for her to enter. Then he led Apollo through, closed the gate and remounted. "Ready?"

"Ready."

Roark started walking Apollo. "I've got a special place to show you."

"Okay, let's go."

He grinned and patted his horse. "Okay, Apollo, let's run."

The horse lifted his head and then took off like someone fired a shot.

Sunny followed suit.

Jessica got her saddle seat and leaned down over the saddle, making herself as small as possible, so it was easier for Sunny to run faster. She whooped with joy. As she came up to Roark's side, she laughed. Then she realized she didn't know where they were going. Jessica sat up and slowed to a walk, letting Sunny rest and catch her breath. She didn't like to run a horse until they were exhausted.

He slowed, too, and fell back beside her. "Having fun?"

She grinned and gestured, taking in the

surrounding pasture. "It's wonderful. All this open land to ride in. And you've got forest, too."

"The forest is where we're going. I have a spot there that is perfect for fly-fishing and for camping."

She frowned slightly. "I don't know. I thought I'd want to go camping, but that's another decision and I'm not sure I'm ready to make it. It will put us in very close proximity for four days…and three nights. It will also mess up my writing schedule. I don't build a lot of extra time into my schedule."

He rode closer to her. "Will you just think about it? You can give me your answer on Sunday. If it's yes, we'll head out on Monday and stay out there until Thursday morning. Or Wednesday morning, whatever you want. Just think about it, please?"

She closed her eyes for a moment and then nodded. "I'll think about it."

"Come on, I'll show you. I think the site itself will convince you to come back."

"I brought my fly rod. It's bamboo and was my father's. I admit, I would really like to try it out."

"Did you know most fly rods used to be made of cane? I think they're plastic now. But a bamboo rod," he whistled. "They have to be ordered from an independent maker. I know I've ordered a couple. They're expensive, too. They start at about six-hundred dollars and run into the thousands."

"I know. I've had offers for Dad's rod, but I'll never sell it. I would have to be very desperate to even consider it."

"I won't let you get that desperate."

"You can't say that. Who knows where we'll be by that time?"

"I know."

She gritted her teeth for a moment. With her eyes narrowed, she lit into him. "How can you be so arrogant? We've only known each other for a week. Are you saying you already know—" She stopped short, remembering how she felt when she first met him. The awareness of someone she'd never known before. The feeling that he was the one for her. The electricity that traveled through her when they kissed. "I'm just saying we don't know for sure."

Roark pulled to a stop.

She did, too.

He dismounted and let the reins fall to the ground, then he walked over to her. He took the reins from her hands and let them fall.

They must train both Sunny and Apollo not to move when the reins were on the ground. She knew from experience it took patience with the horse to get them to do this.

Roark reached up and lifted Jessica to the ground, but didn't remove his hands from her waist. Instead, he wrapped her in his arms. "I want you more than I've ever wanted anyone in my life. I know it's too soon to tell you my feelings, but be aware they are real. I'm not playing games. Not with you. Not about this. Not about us."

Jessica looked up at him. "I can't fall in love with you. I don't…I won't let myself hurt like that again."

"Tell me what happened, please, if it's not too hard for you.".

She pulled out of his arms and turned her back to him. "I was engaged to a man named Joseph Redding. We were supposed to get married the next year, but he left me, though I didn't know it at the time. He and my best friend, a woman named Mandy, were in a car accident and died. I've always felt a little guilty because when I found out, I was almost glad. They'd gotten what they deserved. And that's so wrong. They didn't deserve to die."

"Jessica, look at me." He took her in his arms again.

She still kept her gaze on the ground.

"You did nothing wrong. It's normal to feel that way about someone you love, leaving you. Honey, look at me."

She finally looked up. "I will never cheat on you or make you feel like anything less than the most amazing woman that you are."

"I wish I could believe you—"

"You can. Please, just try." He leaned down and kissed her. He moved from her lips to her neck.

She rolled her head to the side, exposing her skin to his kisses.

He didn't disappoint, raining fiery kisses up and down the side of her neck.

Jessica moaned, and her knees collapsed.

Roark held her safe, never letting her fall.

She clasped her arms around his neck. "Oh, Roark. You make it so hard to resist you."

"That's the idea, sweetheart. I don't want you to resist me. I don't want you to *want* to resist me."

With her heart hammering, she raised her lips to his. "Kiss me. Really kiss me, like you mean all the words you're saying."

He studied her face. "Jessica. I do mean all the words I'm saying. I won't ever lie to you. Never."

She closed her eyes and thought a minute. *Can I trust him or believe him? How will I know if I don't give him the chance? I'll go on the camping trip. If nothing else, I'll get in some fishing.* "I want to believe you. I do. Let's revisit this after the camping trip."

He kissed her again. "You're staying? Thank God. I'm in favor of anything that means you'll give me a chance."

She reached up and cupped one side of his face. "We'll see if we can't work this out." Standing on her tiptoes, she kissed him, deeply with all the love—yes, love—she felt for him. But she couldn't stand on just love. She thought she'd loved Joseph, and yet, now she knew what she felt for him was so far away from true love. So far removed from what she felt for Roark, how could she even compare the two?

"As much as I'd like to do this all day, I really want you to see the place I want to bring us to camp."

"Okay. Let's mount up." She put her left foot in the stirrup and bounced on her right leg just enough to give her a little lift, so she was up and her right leg was over the saddle. She sat and put her right foot into its stirrup. She smiled, still amazed she remembered how to mount.

"Ready?"

"I was born ready."

He laughed. "Okay, Miss Kirby. Let's gallop to the tree line, then we'll have to walk through the trees. There's not really a path. You'll just have to follow my lead."

"Ready? Let's go." She tapped Sunny's sides, and the horse started trotting. Jessica kept tapping until Sunny was galloping as fast as she could go. Jessica couldn't help it. She whooped again.

Roark laughed and caught up to her and then passed her…easily.

He'd been holding Apollo back, that jerk. She didn't want to win except by her and Sunny's abilities. She leaned over the saddle and talked to the horse. "Sunny, girl time to prove your son is not better than you. Come on now, let's go."

The horse took off like a streak. She still had a lot of power. Sunny caught her colt in no time and pulled ahead.

Roark wasn't laughing now. He had Apollo going at full speed.

Sunny was, too…now.

Jessica should have let her run as fast as she wanted before. Not that it mattered, because the tree line was coming up fast.

She and Sunny reached the tree line and came to a stop.

Roark and Apollo were just a second or two behind...but still behind.

Jessica laughed. Her heart was light, and she admitted she was having the time of her life...with Roark. She didn't care about his money.

Roark would not understand when she told him she wanted nothing to do with his money. He thought everyone wanted his money, but she didn't. She knew people came out of the woodwork to borrow money, or to just have him give them money, because he could afford it. She didn't want to be one of those people, someone who used him for his money.

She might not be wealthy, but she owned her home and made enough to live comfortably. Some months, she even put some in savings. Jessica was interested in the man. Was he her Prince Charming? She could use this in a book. How would she end it? What sort of suspense would she have in the novel? She always put some suspense in her books, even if it was just a little who-done-it, like someone was stealing hay for their parents whose ranch was failing...or...

"Jessica?"

She turned toward him and blinked several times. "What? Oh, I'm sorry. My mind was wandering, going over a plot for a book. That's the bane of an author's life...the imagination is always going. So, where is this camping spot?"

"Right this way." He turned Apollo, so they

skimmed along the edge of the forest for a bit, and then he turned onto the skinniest path into the forest.

Clearly, no one came this way very often. It was only wide enough for one horse at a time, so Jessica followed Roark. They walked the horses through trees so thick she felt them closing in around her.

Shortly, the path gave way to a lush green meadow surrounded by the dense forest she'd just ridden through. It thrilled her to see the unobstructed blue sky again.

"Come this way." He waved his arm and rode toward the other side of the field.

Jessica followed, and when she reached the other side, she heard the sounds of rushing water. "Roark, listen." She shouted as she rode in the sound's direction.

At the edge of the meadow, a stream rushed past, tumbling over rocks along the way. She dismounted and walked down to the edge of the water, where she had a good view up and down the creek. She squatted, cupped her hand, and dipped it into the water. The liquid was perfectly clear, and she was suddenly very thirsty. She brought her hand up and sipped. The water was cool, not icy, but still very refreshing.

Standing, she walked back up the hill to where Roark sat on Apollo. "What feeds this stream?"

"An underground lake. It's quite clean, and the fish like it." He pointed downstream. "A perfect spot for fly-fishing is down there, just around the bend."

"I'd love to take a walk along the bank and get a look at it."

"Let's go then." He dismounted and dropped his reins on the ground.

This was the second time she'd seen him do it and she just had to mention it. "It's amazing that your horses are trained to ground tie. They train very few horses that way any longer."

"As you can see, I have a lot of land where there is nowhere to tie a horse, so ground tying was a necessity."

"I can understand that. It's also a nice convenience." She started walking. "Come on. I want to see this fly-fishing spot."

"Right this way, sweetheart."

There it was again. He called me sweetheart. Does he mean it as an endearment or something else? She walked along the bank until she reached the bend. Then she cut the corner to pass the bend in the river. Before her was a beautiful, calm and deep pool. "You were right. It's perfect to fish from the bank or go down to the shore, but it looks too deep to wade."

"It is, but it's perfect for a swim."

She shook her head. "Oh, no, I don't do swimming in cold water."

"Didn't I tell you, there's a hot spring that meets it? The water is quite mild here."

"Really? You're not saying that just so you can see me naked?"

"Well, I'd like to see you naked." He waggled his

brows and grinned. "But I'm not kidding about the creek. It really is nice and refreshing."

"Okay, maybe I'll try it...next time."

He laughed. "Going to pack your swimsuit?"

"That's the plan." She grinned and turned back toward the horses. The sun was setting and she shivered in the light breeze. "I suppose we should head back to the ranch. When did you plan on coming back to camp?"

"I thought we could spend today and tomorrow at the ranch and come back here on Sunday. Does that meet with your approval?"

"Yes, that'll work. Speaking of which, I need to do a little work while I'm here. I'll try to do that tonight after we go to bed." *I need to write chapter fourteen and then the epilogue, and I'll be done with that book. I can probably format it and upload it tomorrow. Then I can start on my next series. I think I'll set it on a ranch in Montana.*

Roark lifted his brows. "So we're going to bed... together?" He winked.

She felt her face heat centered in her cheeks. "Not together...together. Together...apart."

He laughed and put an arm around her shoulders. "I'm teasing you, but I won't turn you down...when you're ready."

"I'll remember that."

I don't understand myself. Why do I feel so comfortable with Roark? Why do I want to drop my clothes and let him make love to me? I know I can't. I won't be put in that position again. I will not let myself be hurt, and I'm afraid Roark could hurt me deeply because I care for him more than I've ever cared for a man and more than I want to admit.

* * *

THE NEXT DAY, they rode back to the stream. Jessica brought her flyrod and fishing vest. The vest held flies that her father had tied. She hadn't been able to actually use the flyrod or the flies in ten years. It was time that she honored her father by indulging in one of his favorite pastimes, one he'd done with her.

Roark brought his flyrod, too.

"Are we keeping or releasing?"

He looked up. "I think we should release them since we aren't camping and have no way of preparing them."

"Okay. Good to know."

She fished in the pool, and he fished in the creek below it.

Jessica hadn't finished reeling in her second cast when a fish hit her Royal Coachman fly. She pulled the tip of her rod up and set the hook. "Fish on!" She shouted as she reeled in, keeping steady pressure on the line so the fish didn't have a chance to spit out the hook.

When she got it nearly up to the shore, she used her net and scooped the beautiful brook trout out of the water. She cradled the fish and removed the fly, then released the fish back into the water. "Live to be caught another day, my friend."

Roark came up beside her and laughed. "You talk to the fish?"

"Of course. Don't you? I want to be on good footing with them so they bite my fly again and again. One of these days, I'll keep him and he'll make a delightful meal for us."

"I'm glad you said for us. I didn't have any luck. Are you about ready to explore a bit? I have a little hike we can go on if you're up to it."

"That sounds great. I love to hike. Where are we going?"

He pointed to the west toward the mountains. "To where the spring exits the rocks. It's over the hill and it's a bit of a climb but really easy walking. Are you ready for that?"

She put her hands in her back pockets. "Sure. I don't mind a little rock climbing."

"There is only one place that is a little dangerous, and that's only if you fall. We take a path along the rock face over the stream to get to the other side and the outlet for the creek."

"Okay. I'll be careful."

They started off following the stream as it headed first north and then west. About half an hour after they started, they came to the path over the rock face he'd told her about.

He went first. "Just walk where I do and you'll be fine."

She followed him. Suddenly, her boot slipped on some loose gravel. "Roark!"

* * *

He stopped and called over the side. "Jessica! Jessica!"

"I'm here. There is a small ledge that I landed on, but I've twisted my ankle. I can't climb up."

He laid on the ground and peered over the side. He saw her boots on the edge of the ledge but couldn't see the rest of her. "I need a rope to get to you. I'm going to have to go for help."

"Okay. You better get started."

"It will probably be after dark before I get back. Will you be all right until then?"

"I'm fine. No animal can get to me, so I'm perfectly safe until you return."

"I'll hurry. I've got a satellite phone in my saddle-bags for an emergency. I'll have to wait for them. The only place they can land is in the meadow, and then I'll bring them back here."

"Okay. I'll see you when you return. And Roark?"

"Yes."

"Try to hurry. My ankle is killing me."

"I'll hurry, baby. As fast as I can. I'm leaving now."

"Understood."

He ran as fast as he could, safely off the cliff, and picked up speed as he went. When he finally reached Apollo, he opened his saddlebags and pulled out the sat phone. "He dialed the house."

"Sullivan residence."

"Athena. It's Roark. There has been an accident. Jessica slipped and is about twenty feet below the path.

Tell Jubal that I'm at my camping spot. He'll know where that is. Get a copter here as soon as possible."

"It might be faster if Mannie flies up and gets you to take her to the hospital. Then you could go together."

"Good idea. Get Mannie up here and send an Ace bandage so I can wrap it and hopefully give her some relief from the pain."

"Will do. You can expect Mannie in about fifteen minutes."

"I'll be waiting." He signed off.

Roark thought about going back up to be with Jessica, but he'd miss Mannie if he did. It was better if he waited. He paced around the meadow. From tree line to tree line, straight across the meadow and back. He lost count of how many repetitions he'd done by the time he heard the whirr of the chopper blades.

Mannie landed in the middle of the meadow.

Jubal jumped out and ran to Roark, carrying a rope, a harness, and an Ace bandage. "Here you go, Boss. Where is she?"

"Follow me. How much rope did you bring?"

"One-hundred yards."

Roark was huffing as he ran toward the rocks and the climb. *It's getting dark. I need to get her now.*

He and Jubal reached the site.

Roark called over the side. "Jessica? How you doing, baby?"

"I'm still here and I'm doing fine, but I wouldn't turn down a Vicodin right about now."

"Can you put on a harness and we can haul you up?"

He looked over at Jubal, who was tying the rope off to a pine tree. It would hold strong.

"I can't. I'm unable to maneuver on this ledge."

"Okay, sweetie. I'll come down and get you. Do you trust me?"

"Do I have a choice?"

He chuckled. "No, babe you don't." He turned to Jubal. "Can you haul us up alone?"

"As long as you're helping, I can do it. Or I can keep the rope taut if you climb it. It's up to you, Roark."

"I can probably climb, and that will be easier on you. If you looped the rope around you and back up as I climb, we'll have her up in no time."

Jubal nodded. "Okay, let's do this."

Roark watched as he wrapped the rope around his waist three times. Roark knew it was three times, so it wouldn't get too tight as he hauled Roark and Jessica up from the ledge.

He lowered himself on the rope to the ledge Jessica was on. Looking at it he cringed. It was a miracle she'd landed there and not missed it entirely. "Jessica, honey, can you stand?"

"Yes, give me a minute."

"I can help if it would be easier."

"No, I don't think it would be easier," she snapped.

He realized she wasn't furious with him, but with the situation. It was out of her control, and she didn't like it one bit.

She stood by using the rock face and finding finger holds to pull herself up."

"That's great. I'm going to lean down until I'm the same height as a large dog. I need you to get on my back, wrap your legs around my waist, and your arms around my neck. Just don't squeeze me too tight. I need to breathe."

"Okay. I can do that."

Once he and Jessica were ready, he pulled on the rope and shouted for Jubal. "We're ready. I'm starting my climb." He pulled himself up, with Jessica on his back, hand over hand. The time went by slowly, even though Jubal was pulling the rope up, too. Finally, they reached the top.

Jubal didn't stop pulling them until Roark was away from the edge. He kept the rope tight until Roark said otherwise.

Roark lifted himself to his knees, with her on his back, until she could roll off him without hurting her ankle.

Jubal came over and helped her get completely off Roark's back.

"Okay." Roark stood and looked at Jessica. "Let's get back to the copter and get you to the hospital."

"Yes. How far is the helicopter from here?" She leaned against Jubal.

Roark stood and came over to her. "It's in the meadow about thirty minutes from here."

"It will take me a lot longer, even with you and Jubal, to help me." She tried to stand on her good leg, but it was too much.

"No, it won't." Suddenly, Roark walked over to her

and scooped her into his arms.

"No, Roark. You can't carry me all that way."

"Yes, I can. Trust me...again. Can you do that?"

She didn't answer for a moment.

He wondered if she'd say no and he'd have to override her and carry her, anyway. Having her cooperation would make it much easier for everyone.

"All right, but when you need to rest, you have to stop."

"Done. Let's start with you on my back, like we did on the way up the cliff face."

She nodded.

Roark let her out of his arms, but held her enough to support her if need be.

Jubal helped her onto Roark's back.

"I'm starting down. Would you bring the rope and catch up, please?" Roark looked over at Jubal.

Jubal nodded. "I'll be right behind you.

Roark took off walking.

After forty-five minutes and several stops, he, Jessica and Jubal all reached the meadow.

As they started toward the copter, Mannie started it and the engine roared to life.

Roark set Jessica into the copter in the seat behind Mannie.

She buckled the seat belt.

He checked it, found it tight and went around the copter and got in beside her.

Jubal stayed with the horses and rode back to the house.

The helicopter lifted off the ground and headed toward Bozeman Health Deaconess Regional Medical Center.

Mannie contacted the hospital. "Bozeman, this is Sullivan International helicopter two. We're on the way in with a woman who sustained injuries in a fall off a cliff. Injuries include a sprained ankle, facial bruising and perhaps a concussion."

"Got it, Sullivan. We'll be ready. Bozeman, out."

Upon arrival, they were met by a team from the ER.

A nurse came over to Roark. "We'll take her from here, Mr. Sullivan. Given the nature of her fall, we'd like to do a full workup."

Roark turned to Jessica. "Does that meet with your permission?"

"Yes. That would be fine."

The nurse looked up at Roark. "Very well. We'll see you inside."

Two orderlies, one on either end, guided the gurney into the ER.

Roark turned toward Mannie. "Come in after you've moved the helicopter."

"Yes, sir. I'll also call the house and let Athena know what's happening."

"Great. Thanks."

"Sure. See you inside."

I followed Jessica into the ER and wondered if she'd be okay. Would she call off their week in Montana? Perhaps she'd stay and I could help her heal. Or would she decide that being in a relationship with me is too hard?

CHAPTER 9

𝒶 week later

JESSICA TRIED to get around without her crutches, but it hurt too much. Regardless of how much it hurt, she needed to get back home. She enjoyed being close to Roark, but she disliked being waited on hand and foot.

Roark entered the den where Jessica now slept so she wouldn't have to do the stairs.

She looked up. "I'm glad you're here. Take a seat."

He sat in the chair behind the desk instead of the chair near the sofa. She thought that was telling. He always needed to be in charge. "Roark. I want to go home."

"You'll heal better here. We can get you anything you need."

"That's the point. I don't want to be waited on. I

need to do things by myself, and I need to sleep in a proper bed. My bed."

He stood and walked over to her. "I can take you to PT. How will you do that at your home?"

"I don't know, but I'll figure it out. It's my left ankle. I can probably drive myself. Or I can take a cab. The point is, I'll do it on my own."

"I don't like it. I don't like you being alone."

She patted the seat beside her on the sofa. "Sit."

He did and placed his left arm around her shoulders. "I'm not going to win this one, am I?"

"Nope."

"What can I do, to help you?"

"Nothing. Just take me home."

He squeezed her shoulders. "All right. I'll arrange it for tomorrow."

"Thank you."

He turned her toward him. "You're good for me, Jessica Kirby." He lowered his head and took her lips with his.

The kiss was passionate, and she felt it deep, all the way to her toes. Her insides turned liquid and pooled between her legs. She was hot. He surrounded her and held her tight. She raised her arms and placed them around his neck, pulling him tighter to her. She needed him…needed this. It had been so long since she felt like this, felt like someone really wanted *her* and cared about *her*.

But it was so soon. This couldn't be happening now. They'd only known each other for about three weeks and for half of that, she was laid up with a sprained ankle. How could this be? How could she feel like this? Were these feelings real or was she just enamored with him because he was with her and *wanted* to be with *her*, not someone he imagined her to be? She hadn't trusted anyone since Joseph's betrayal and death over three years ago.

But now she knew she was in love with Roark. How could that be? But if it wasn't love, what was it? Lust? Would this feeling go away if she slept with him? No. She was sure it wouldn't and the feelings might even grow stronger, but she wasn't ready to find out either way.

Roark pulled back. "I think I lost you somewhere."

"I'm sorry. Arguing with—never mind, it's silly."

"I'll get you home tomorrow. Today, Mannie, Jubal, and I are looking for rustlers in the copter. A couple of my cowboys were shot at, and I want to know if it was because someone is rustling my cattle. After that, we'll get back to this conversation and what you were arguing with yourself about."

"It wasn't very interesting. Go on and find the rustlers. They need to be stopped. Not only because they are stealing from you, but you know they are stealing from little ranchers, too. Ranchers who can't afford the loss, like you can. So, go get them. Stop them."

He gave her a kiss, a light one on the lips. Then he stood. "I'll be back."

* * *

"I'M TELLING YOU, someone cut the fence. On the north side 'bout as far from the house as you can get."

"We're taking the copter to see if we can spot any rustlers," said Mannie.

"I'm going with you." Jubal looked at the cowboy. "Did you see anything else besides the fence down?"

"Yeah, there's four-wheeler tracks all over the place, and I didn't make them. I was on horseback."

"Okay, go on and finish with your horse." Jubal jutted his chin toward the bay that was standing by a stall, with the saddle half off. "Then cleanup for supper."

"Yes, sir." The cowboy walked away.

Roark stepped forward. "Let's go now before we lose the daylight." He clapped Mannie on the back. "You ready to fly?"

He grinned. "Sure thing, boss."

"We'll find the rustlers, Roark. And we'll shut them down." Mannie punched his right fist into his left palm.

"We will. But not today. This is just for recognizance."

"Gotcha," said Mannie.

"Okay, let's go see if we can find those rustlers. The sheriff will be glad for the information." Roark took off toward the helicopter's hangar.

* * *

JESSICA WALKED with her crutches into the kitchen. She found Athena snapping green beans.

Athena looked up and her eyes narrowed. "You shouldn't be up. You need to keep that leg up."

Jessica waved off her concern. "I'm fine, but I am going crazy. My book isn't going the way I want it to. I need a break from it. Why don't you let me help you with the beans? I can prop my leg on a chair. With all the cowboys eating here, you'll need lots of them." She made her way to the sink and washed her hands.

"That's true, and it will give us a chance to get to know each other. We haven't had any time alone together. I understand you're a writer. What do you write?"

"I write historical and contemporary western romance novels."

Athena's eyes lit up. "You do? I love to read western romance. Usually historical, but I'm open to contemporary, too."

"Good, because I write both, plus I've written some scifi romance, but I don't do that anymore. I'm just getting into contemporary. In some ways, it's easier because I don't have to do as much research, but surprisingly, I still have to do some. I have to research the area where I'm setting the novel. For instance, I've never been to Montana before, but now I know what it looks like other than just in pictures. It's much more fun to visit and know the country in person."

"I imagine it would be. I'd love to go visit other

countries and then write about them." Athena sighed and took a deep breath.

"Why don't you? You and Jubal must get vacation time. Go see somewhere you've always wanted to see." She put the paper towel she dried her hands with in the trash under the sink and then walked to the table and sat.

"That's easier said than done."

"Why? I'm sure Roark would send you wherever you want to go on his plane. I get the feeling you and Jubal are very important to him and for more reasons than you are top-notch employees."

Athena blushed but smiled. "He's important to us, too, and he knows that. It's not the money. Jubal doesn't like to travel. He's perfectly happy just going fishing. Let me get a chair, so you can keep your leg up." Athena grabbed a chair and arranged it for Jessica.

Jessica put her leg up on the chair. She had to admit her ankle felt better up. When it was down, she felt the blood pounding through it. "Well, go fishing someplace else. Go to Alaska and do salmon fishing or deep sea fishing off California or Mexico or Florida or in Hawaii. I caught a sailfish once while off the big island of Hawaii. It was so much fun. It was just like on those fishing shows where it jumps out of the water and dances." She bent her arm at the elbow and moved it in a wavy motion up and down.

Athena thought for a minute. "Hmm. I might convince him to do that."

Jessica grinned. "Don't know until you try. How long have you two been married?"

"Nearly thirty years." Athena got her a bowl for the snapped beans.

"And in all that time, you've never gone anywhere you want to?"

"It's not as simple as that."

"But it is." Jessica took a bunch of beans and started snapping them into the bowl. "My dad was the adventurous one in the family. Like Jubal, he loved to hunt and fish, but he also wanted to see the world. Mom was perfectly happy staying at home, and so neither of them did the traveling he wanted to. Now, she wishes she had that time to live over. She'd go with him anywhere he wanted, just to be with him. You should do things before it's too late."

Athena stood and put her arms around Jessica and before fetching her the box of tissues from the counter.

Suddenly, Jessica realized she was crying. She pulled a tissue from the box and dried her eyes, then blew her nose. "Thank you. I hadn't realized I still missed him so much. I think about him every day and wish he was here to tease me about my books and to finally convince Mom to go with him to Europe or Australia or Ireland. Somewhere other than our hometown of Golden, a suburb of Denver."

Athena embraced her again. "How long has he been gone?"

She loved that Athena just held her and let her talk. "Ten years, though when I think about him, it seems like only yesterday. To me, he's still alive." She touched her chest over her heart. "In here."

Athena squeezed her shoulders. "Good. I'm glad. That's what matters now."

"Yes, it does. Shall we get these beans snapped so we can get to the rest of them? Because I know, with all those mouths you have to feed, this is not the whole batch."

Athena laughed.

The sound reminded her of her mother…in happier times.

"You're right. This is half, but if I cook them together, the cowboys will take everything. They don't know how to stop. They are more like teenage boys that way. Cowboys are always hungry because they work so hard."

Jessica laughed. "You're probably right. What is the old saying? 'The only difference between men and boys is the price of their toys.'"

Roark entered from the backyard, followed by Jubal and Mannie. "Are we being disparaged?"

"Sheesh!" Jessica jumped and nearly spilled her bowl of beans on the floor. "You scared the bejeepers out of me."

Roark raised one of his perfect black brows and crossed his arms over his muscled chest. "Bejeepers?"

Jubal laughed.

So did Mannie, who tried to cover it with a cough and a hand over his mouth.

She turned, stood and grabbed her crutches, then

she made her way over to him and poked him in the chest. "Don't think you can make fun of me and get out of this. You shouldn't sneak up on us."

He raised his hands in surrender. "Okay. I'll be louder next time I come in from outside."

"That's right." Her lips quivered, and she started to laugh.

Then Athena laughed.

Jubal shook his head. "Ya'all are crazy."

Mannie looked at all of them. "I think you've lost it. I'm headed home."

Jessica stood in front of Roark, facing the others in the room.

He wrapped his arms around the top of her shoulders.

"Mannie, why don't you bring Alice to dinner? I'd love to meet her."

Roark looked at his foreman. "Of course, I would love to meet her myself. Come to dinner."

Mannie hmmm and shuffled his boots. "I don't know. She's probably made dinner already. She likes to spoil me that way."

"Then come for coffee and dessert," said Jessica.

Mannie nodded. "Sure, sure, that would be great. We'll see you about seven this evening."

"Sounds good." Roark lowered his arms and watched Mannie leave. Then he walked to the cupboard, got a coffee mug, and poured himself a cup of hot coffee.

Roark rested his forearms on the top of the back of

a chair. "Now, Jessica, why did we just invite Mannie and his fiancée to coffee?"

She grasped her crutches. "Because I want to meet the woman who has agreed to marry a man twenty years her senior."

He set the mug on the counter and walked closer. Frowning, he looked down at her. "I thought you said age doesn't matter."

She reached up and cupped his face. "It doesn't...to me...and maybe not to her either. But I think it must to Mannie, or he would have brought her around before now." She turned to Athena and Jubal. "Have you two met Alice?"

Athena shook her head. "I didn't even know Mannie had a girlfriend, much less a fiancée."

"Exactly my point." She looked up at Roark and put her hands on her hips. "I don't know Mannie at all, but it surprised me you weren't aware he was engaged. I would have thought you would know that information through Athena and Jubal, if not through Mannie."

"I see what you're getting at. I just thought I'd been more distracted than usual." He winked.

Heat rose up her face, and she knew the pink color went with it. "Be that as it may, you keep better track of your employees than anybody I've ever known."

Roark let out a sigh. "Well, let's get dinner over. Athena, can we help in any way?"

She looked at Roark, her perfectly plucked and penciled eyebrows lifted before she narrowed her eyes and frowned. "Have I ever needed your help in the kitchen, Roark Sullivan? Or you, Jubal Mack?"

Jubal lifted his arms, hands palms out. "Don't look at me. I didn't offer. I'm grabbing a beer, just like always, and then I'm going to sit on the porch."

He walked to the huge refrigerator with the freezer on the bottom and a large upper door. It was the 'fridge Jessica wanted in her house when she needed a new one. She couldn't see spending the money when she had a perfectly good refrigerator at home.

"You all get out of the kitchen so I can continue. I have my way of doing things, and that doesn't include any of you." She smiled at Jessica. "That includes you, sweetie. Thank you for helping me with the beans, but now go sit with these...men...and figure how to help them. If the rustlers shoot at people, it won't be long before someone gets hurt and maybe killed." She gazed at Roark. "You have to stop it before that happens."

Roark looked around the kitchen, his gaze landing first on Jubal, then Athena, and finally on Jessica. "Athena is right. We have to stop this...now." He took Jessica's hands. "I don't know what I'd do if anything happened to you."

She looked up at him. He was as serious as a heart attack as her father would have said, and that realization scared her.

CHAPTER 10

*A*fter dinner that night, Jessica walked into the living room on her crutches.

Roark stood next to her.

Mannie and Alice came at seven as arranged.

Roark invited them in and shut the door behind them.

Jubal and Athena rounded out the group.

Alice had dyed blonde hair, was about five feet, six inches tall and was very curvy, with a large bosom and narrow hips. She wore a lot of makeup, which made telling her age difficult, so they had to take Mannie's word that she was twenty years younger than him.

Mannie smiled widely, obviously proud.

"This is my fiancée, Alice Nelson. We met at the Silver Dollar. She was my favorite waitress, and she finally agreed to go out with me about three months ago. We hit it off right away. Can you believe it?"

Jessica stepped forward from the little group that

had gathered for coffee that night. "Hi." She put out her hand. "I'm Jessica Kirby. I—"

Alice's eyes widened. "Oh, my gosh. Jessica Kirby, the author? I love your books. You are the reason I read." Alice grabbed Jessica's hand and pumped it before pulling her into a hug. She released her. "I can't believe I'm meeting my favorite author."

Jessica was happy to be recognized. She didn't do book tours and so didn't often meet fans. "I'm very flattered. As a matter of fact, you made my day."

Roark chuckled. "And here I thought I made your day."

Jessica turned toward Roark. "You always say I've made your day." She blew him a kiss.

His emerald eyes flashed wide, and he pretended to catch the kiss with his hand.

Jessica grinned. *That should keep you wondering.*

Everyone else introduced themselves and they all shook hands.

After that was complete, Athena pointed toward the door. "Let's sit where we can talk. Roark, will you help me with the coffee, please?"

He smiled. "Of course." Roark took Jessica in his arms and kissed her. "We'll be out in a few minutes."

She heard laughter and giggles from behind them.

He released her, dropped his chin to his chest and then sighed. Then he raised his head enough to see her and grinned. "They are such children."

Jessica laughed. "Go on."

He followed Athena to the kitchen.

Athena returned with a tray with the coffee and cups.

Roark did the same with the tray of coffeecake and plates. "We're back. Athena has the coffee. Clear the coffee table."

Jessica had made herself comfortable on the sofa with her leg extended over the sofa cushions so her foot was elevated. Now, however, she put her foot on the floor so Roark could sit next to her. "Clear the coffee table. They're back."

Mannie and Alice sat on a beautiful log sofa with the pillows made from suede leather in a soft beige color, directly across from Roark and Jessica.

Jubal sat in one of the dark brown suede wing chairs, which were placed on the long ends of the rectangular coffee table between them all.

"You're already giving orders." Roark smiled.

"Yeah, you are," said Mannie without a smile.

Jessica reared her head back slightly, like she'd been slapped. This was the first clue she'd gotten that Mannie didn't like her...and she didn't know why. Rather than Alice, could it be Mannie who was the problem?

"I'm sorry, Mannie. I meant no offense." She sat next to Roark, leaving enough room for Athena to sit next to her and to Jubal in the chair on that end.

Mannie glanced at Roark, and suddenly the old Mannie was back. The man who'd liked her well enough when they were talking about going up in the helicopter. *Was that just for Roark's benefit? Does the real Mannie dislike me?*

"I'm sorry, Jessica. Just a little nervous about tomorrow." He gave her a small laugh. "Flying the boss always makes my stomach turn upside down."

Roark put his arm along her shoulders.

She leaned into him. "No worries, Mannie. I'm a little nervous for you all, myself."

Mannie smiled. "I promise to bring the 'copter back safely."

"I'm glad to hear it." She smiled while she said it. She wondered if anyone realized the smile was fake and didn't reach her eyes? Why didn't Mannie like her? She hadn't picked up on that when they first met, but he was almost hostile now. Had she done something to irritate him? Perhaps when she invited him and Alice for dinner? Was that what set him off? But why would that be?

Jessica tried to ignore Mannie. "So, Alice, why don't you tell us a little about yourself? I know you like to read my books, and that is the best thing as far as I'm concerned. But what else should we know about Alice Nelson? Do you have any siblings?"

Alice's smile never faded. "I do. I'm the middle child of five. Four boys and me. They spoiled me rotten." She laughed and leaned back against the sofa, with her hand on Mannie's knee. "Even my little brothers spoiled me. They took their cue from the older two. Benjamin is thirty-two, Adam, thirty-four, Carson, twenty-nine and David, twenty-seven. My parents kept us all close together. They said it was so we would all have friends to play with."

Athena gazed at Jessica. "Would you cut the cake, please? I'll pour the coffee."

"Sure." Jessica cut six good-sized slices.

Everyone passed each one around until they each had a piece of cake and a mug of coffee.

"Jessica, why don't you tell us a bit about you?" Mannie took a sip of his coffee and looked over the rim of the cup.

Jessica angled her body to face him. "There's not really much to tell. I'm an only child. My father was my idol. He passed away ten years ago. I'm twenty-seven and I write western romance and scifi novels for a living. The industry as a whole, and my books in particular, have been very good to me. I'm able to support myself with my writing, which was always my dream. How many people get to live out their dream?"

"Not many," agreed Roark. "I'm glad you're able to do that and are still happy writing your books."

"Happy? I'm ecstatic." She looked at Roark and then toward Mannie and Alice. "Every time I publish a new book or the print version of an ebook, or the foreign version of one of my books, I smile as I'm doing it. Getting copies of my print books is so gratifying. Holding the book in my hands is even better than the ebook...for the author's morale. It means we're actual authors. No one can deny it." She pretended to clasp a book to her chest while closing her eyes and dropping her head back.

Then she dropped her chin back to normal position and looked at Alice. "And because I love what I do, I'll never work a day in my life...well, from now on. I definitely worked in my previous life before I started writing. I started working for the Golden Chamber of Commerce when I was fifteen in their tourist booth, which was fun. But some of my other jobs sucked. I can honestly say I feel sorry for fast food workers. Having done it, I realize they are under a lot of pressure." She dropped her hands back on her lap. "Alice, are you still working at the Silver Dollar?"

"No, when Mannie asked me to move in, I had to quit. It's too far to drive every day. Especially when tips are bad. Waitresses don't make a lot per hour. They report we make minimum wage, but what that amounts to is four dollars hourly and the rest," she made quotes with her fingers, "is made up with tips. Some nights, we don't even make half of the $9.95 minimum wage." Alice was red in the face by the time she quit talking.

"I'm sorry. I didn't mean to get you upset."

Alice waved her hand. "It's nothing. I'm just angry about our wages. If I thought it would do any good, I'd protest in front of the Silver Dollar. But it won't matter to management and the owners and they'll just take it out on the waitstaff." She sat back, crossed her arms, and put her chin on her chest.

Jessica knew the sign of dismissal. Alice was done with this subject. So, rather than let the discussion fade, Jessica changed topics. "So, what about the rustlers? I didn't think they existed today, but only in the old west."

She watched Alice lift her head; her interest piqued. *Good. Good. I want to know what you know about the rustlers, and I hope you are not just using Mannie.*

Roark sat forward and set his empty plate on the coffee table. "Rustlers are still around. They never actually went away... just their methods of stealing changed. Instead of riding horses, now they use four wheelers. Before that, they used trucks, small ones like you'd rent to move from one loft to another. They'd drive up to the fence, cut it, and then herd the animals they'd previously collected into the truck with a couple of cowboys on horses. Smart rustlers repaired the fence, to a degree, so the rancher wouldn't notice until he counted his cattle. Nowadays, they don't bother. They're gone by the time we find the cut fence."

Jessica watched his hands form into fists. She reached over, placed a hand on his knee, and gave it a little squeeze.

He swung his gaze to hers. His brows curled down, and his eyes showed he was troubled by more than anger. As he looked at her, his face softened and his hands relaxed. "I'm sorry. I'm just frustrated, that's all."

"I'm sure we all are." Jubal reached over and put his hand on top of Athena's where it rested on the arm of the sofa. "This isn't just a crime against you, Roark. It's a crime against everyone at the ranch."

"Why do you say that?" Alice's eyes narrowed and her brunette brows formed a slash above her eyes.

"Because this ranch is our bread and butter. If the cattle continue to disappear, Roark could decide to sell it rather than take substantial losses."

Roark nodded.

"That's not to say he would," continued Jubal. "But he might, and if we can't find the rustlers and stop the cattle from disappearing, I wouldn't blame him if he does."

Jessica watched Mannie and Alice. They looked at each other, and she knew in that instant that Mannie knew what was happening. He was aware Alice was part of the gang of rustlers and was using him for information.

She didn't know how Mannie knew or for how long he'd known, but he had the knowledge, and he was just letting it happen.

About half an hour later, Mannie scooted to the edge of the sofa. "We need to go. Morning comes early around here."

Jubal nodded and stood. "That it does. We should go, too."

Athena also rose and reached for the tray with the coffee. "I need to clean this up first—"

Reaching out, Jessica placed a hand on her arm. "Don't worry. Roark and I will take care of this." She looked over at Roark. "Won't we?"

"Of course. Go on. All of you. We'll see you in the morning." Roark picked up the coffee tray and the cake tray, too, with the cake tray on the bottom.

Jessica stood. "Good night, all."

The two couples left through the kitchen.

Jessica followed them on her crutches.

Roark followed her. He set the trays on the counter by the sink. "Do we really have to do the dishes? I was hoping for some time on the porch swing, just the two of us…watching the stars…or other things."

She smiled. "You are a wicked man, Mr. Sullivan, and yes, we have to do the dishes. I'll load the dishwasher and you empty the coffee pots and put the cream in the fridge. I didn't say it would be perfect. We'll do what we can."

Fifteen minutes later, Jessica was drying her hands with a dish towel. "There. All done."

Roark came up and put his arms around her waist.

She placed hers around his neck and balanced on her good leg.

"So, Miss Kirby, how about that porch now?"

Jessica grinned. "I'd love to, Mr. Sullivan. Will I need a jacket?"

"No, I'll keep you warm." He leaned down and gave her a quick peck on the lips. "Let's go." He let go of her only long enough to lift her into his arms.

Jessica wrapped her arms around his neck. "What about my crutches?"

"I'm your crutches tonight."

He worked his way through the living room, into the foyer and out the dark wood double doors.

"Have I told you how much I like your home? It's beautiful."

He carried her to the swing and set her on it.

Then he sat beside her and tugged her closer. "Can you see yourself ever living here?"

She stiffened for a moment. "I'm not at a point I want to even consider something like that. We've known each other for such a short time. How can you know we'll be compatible? What do we really know about each other?"

"I know enough to know I want to—"

Her heart skipped a beat. "Don't. Please don't say it. Not yet."

"How do you know what I was about to say?"

"Because I have some—maybe the same—feelings, too. What we feel when we're together is amazing, but it's also overwhelming. I need time. I don't want to jump into bed...or into a relationship...without us knowing each other better."

"All right. I understand, and I'll try to control myself and not push you."

They were both quiet for a few minutes.

She laid her head on his chest, then sat up. "Aren't you worried about the rustling?"

"I am."

"And?"

"And I believe it's well in hand."

"I think Mannie has something to do with it, and so does Alice. I think she's getting information from him and sending it to her rustler buddies. I also think Mannie is aware of what she's doing."

He cocked an eyebrow. "You could be a detective.

Do you put in all your novels some suspense? I noticed one in the novel I read."

"Whether it's my historical and contemporary novels, I always put a bit of suspense in them, so I do research. I can't be a detective, but I get a feeling sometimes for…" She shrugged. "Who knows what?"

"Okay, I think you should let this one go."

She sat up straight and turned toward Roark. "But, I can help. Really—"

He held up a hand. "Stop. Let me explain."

"When he realized after she moved in that Alice was using him, he came to me, and we went to see the Gallatin County Sheriff. They're getting very close to arresting all the rustlers."

"I got the distinct feeling Mannie doesn't like me and that was before any mention of rustling cattle was made."

"When all this is over, we'll find out how he really feels. He's a good foreman. I would hate to let him go."

She was aghast. "Why on Earth would you let him go? Because of me? No. I won't have it. I'll feel guilty for the rest of my life if you do that."

"I'll keep Mannie on."

"He's doing a good thing for you, your ranch and all the other ranches this gang has hit."

"He is, and that should be rewarded. I'm glad we see things like this the same."

She sat up straight and then scooted away from him before angling her body back toward him. "You were testing me? That's a terrible thing to do to me." She stood. "I'd like to go to bed now. Maybe I'll see things differently in the morning."

He stood and picked her up. "Okay. I had planned for us to go camping tomorrow, but you're injured, and I don't want to go without you."

"I'm sorry I can't go with you."

They entered the kitchen, and he set her down next to her crutches. "Thank you. Goodnight, Roark."

"Goodnight. Would you like some help to bed?"

"No, thank you. I'm getting good at navigating from the kitchen to the den." She made her way down the hall to the den. Sitting on the sofa, she removed her shoes and then laid back on the blankets. *What am I getting into? Are my feelings for Roark real? How could he feel the same as I do? And yet I feel like he does. He's in love with me. Am I really in love with him? Or am I letting the electricity I feel when we touch cloud my common sense?*

CHAPTER 11

The next morning, after writing for a couple of hours and then having a very troubled sleep, Jessica entered the kitchen for a cup of coffee. The scent of the brew reached her nostrils, and she breathed in the magical smell.

Around the table were five of the cowboys she hadn't met yet, as well as Roark, Jubal, and Athena.

Athena jumped up from the table. "Sit and let me get you a cup of coffee, sweetie."

"Thanks, Athena, I can get it." Jessica was only using one crutch, leaving the other hand free to hold a coffee cup.

"Nonsense. The kitchen is my domain, and just because I might have let you do last night's dishes doesn't mean I'm relinquishing my duties, so sit."

Jessica laughed.

"Did you sleep well?" Roark held his mug with both hands.

"Not really, but I'm better now. Did you go out in the helicopter yet? What did you find?"

"Have your breakfast and then come back to the office. I'll meet you there."

"What do you want for breakfast?" asked Athena.

"Just a bagel and cream cheese, if you have it."

"Sure do. I'll toast it for you."

"That would be great. Thank you, Athena. Usually women are used by men, under their thumb, so to speak, but I don't believe Alice could be under anyone's thumb. I believe she's got Mannie under hers." Jessica sighed. "I know I shouldn't say anything, so forget I did."

"It's all right. I feel the same way. Jubal and I talked last night, and he thinks Mannie is being used, too. The worst thing is that I think he knows it. It's like he's using her in return. I wonder…"

"Wonder what?"

Athena returned to the table with Jessica's coffee and then sat across from her. "I wonder if Mannie was looking for her when he was at the Silver Dollar. It's not a regular haunt for him. He can usually be found at the Bent Branch Saloon. A friend of his owns it."

Jessica narrowed her eyes and furrowed her brows. "So, what was he doing at the Silver Dollar? This gets stranger and stranger by the minute."

"Maybe you'll know more after you talk to Roark in a few minutes."

Jessica wasn't sure. "Yeah, maybe."

Athena smiled. "Sure you will. He wants to be with you too much."

"Do you really think so? I'm afraid we sort of had a fight last night."

"Every couple fights. It's the working it out and then making up that matters." Athena filled a traveling cup with coffee, milk and sugar.

"I suppose that's true. We both seemed to be in a better mood this morning."

"Of course. Now, here's your coffee, just the way you like it."

"Wow, I didn't think anyone was paying attention."

"I always pay attention to guests' requests and needs."

Jessica stood, took the cup from Athena, and put it on the table. Then she wrapped the older woman in her arms. "Thank you."

Athena hugged her back. "You're welcome, sweetie." She pulled out of the hug, but kept her hands on Jessica's shoulders. "Roark has never brought anyone here before. You must be very special."

Jessica shrugged. "I don't know about that. We have something special between us, but I can't put my finger on it. I just don't know what we have. We've only known each other for such a short period of time."

The housekeeper lowered her hands. "Sounds like he's finally found his soulmate. Once you find them, you know, and you'll never let them go. There's something in their touch that travels through you. Did Roark tell you his parents only knew each other for a week before they got married? They've been married now for forty-two years."

Adrenaline made her pulse race. "What? Only a week."

"His mother told me they knew because their touch was electrifying to the other."

"That's the way it is between Roark and me."

"Listen to your heart. It knows."

"Maybe. I don't know, but I've got to go. Thank you."

"You're welcome. Go on, now."

All the way to his office, Jessica thought of nothing but her and Roark. *Do we have the same crazy thing between us that his parents did? Could he really be the one? Could it be we really are soulmates?*

As she approached the office, Roark came toward her, a smile on his face.

"There you are. I wondered if I was going to have to send armed men to retrieve you from Athena."

"She's such a lovely woman."

He took her cup from her and then put her hand in his. "She is. She and Jubal have worked for me for fifteen years...ever since I bought the place. She's been like a mother to me, even though she's not that much older than me. Shall we go?"

"Go where?"

He grinned. "On the helicopter. You want to, don't you?"

"Oh, yes. What about my crutches?"

"You can take them, but I'm carrying you out there."

She tilted her head and shook it no. "Won't Mannie and Jubal be ready to go?"

He waved away her concern. "They can wait. Are you ready? Do you need anything?"

She shook her head. "No, I'm fine. I've got my coffee in a spill proof travel mug, which might turn out to be a really good idea."

"Okay. Let's go." He picked her up and carried her to an immense building.

She'd thought the building was an arena. Apparently, she was wrong. Now that they were getting close, she saw the large doors on one end. "Is the helicopter inside?"

"Yup. This is its home."

"Does it fly out those doors or get rolled out?"

"Neither." He led her into the structure.

The copter sat below an open ceiling.

He stopped.

She looked up. "Oh, my goodness. I never expected the roof to retract. That's a great idea."

"I thought so when I designed it."

Her jaw dropped. "You designed it? Are you an architect, too?"

"Sort of. I know enough to draft the idea of whatever I need. But I let a real architect do the hard lifting with the actual structure and electricity and all the other things that go into building a hangar for a helicopter."

"At least you know your limitations."

"I'd better know them. If I didn't, I could be a

danger to those around me. My design might not withstand the wind and snow if I didn't get expert help."

"When did Mannie learn to fly?"

"As soon as I bought the copter. No one else seemed interested."

"I'm surprised you didn't hire a pilot when you bought it."

"I did. A pilot-slash-instructor. He knew he was only here until Mannie got his license. That was our deal. I paid him a flat rate for twelve months, which is how long he said it would take to get Mannie licensed. For each month less than twelve that it actually took, he got a bonus. The man was motivated, and he got a three months' bonus when he left."

"That's great." She looked at the copter with her stomach in her throat. *Is this really such a good idea?f* "How long ago was that?"

Roark set her down for a minute. She stood with her crutches and watched the helicopter. "You needn't worry. He's been flying for me for about eight years and only crashed once."

With her heart in her throat, she pulled back and looked up at Roark. "What!?"

He laughed again. "I'm teasing. Only about the crash. He really has been flying us around in the 'copter for about eight years, with no crashes."

Jessica released a breath she'd unconsciously been holding. "Thank goodness. You had me second guessing myself. I wasn't going up if he'd crashed. I have a highly developed instinct for survival."

"We'll be just fine. I promise." He crossed his arms over his chest.

She leaned on her crutches with them in her armpits and then wiped imaginary sweat from her forehead. "Good. You have no idea how glad I am to hear that."

Roark laughed and placed his hand on her back, at her waist, while they walked up to the aircraft.

Jubal and Mannie waited outside.

They both smiled, and she thought the smiles looked genuine.

"We heard you holler. Figured Roark must have told you the story about Mannie crashing. He told Athena the same thing, and she refused to get in." Jubal smiled again. "She finally came around. Now, she loves flying around the ranch in it."

"Oh, good." Jessica blew out a breath. "That makes me feel better."

"It's supposed to. Let's get in and get going," said Jubal.

The engines were warming up on the Bell 412 EP.

She knew from the research she'd done for a book this helicopter could cost as much as nine-and-a-half million dollars. But Roark wouldn't even feel a pinch spending that much for one.

Jubal climbed in the front with Mannie.

She and Roark sat in the back.

They all strapped in.

Mannie lifted off, flying out of the hangar through the open roof.

As they rose, she got a wide-open view of the surrounding countryside, which mesmerized her. The rolling hills were covered with meadows of yellow and green grass. Spots of color, which she knew from their horseback ride, were patches of flowers. Copses of pine trees dotted the countryside.

She saw a stream running out of one of them and pointed out the window toward it. "Is that the stream we saw yesterday?"

Roark leaned over and looked through her window. "It is. Good eye." He leaned back. "If *you* don't see signs of rustling, we might not have any going on." He squeezed her knee and winked.

She rolled her eyes and returned her gaze to the landscape below. Suddenly, she saw movement. "Look!" She pointed. Two four-wheelers were herding cattle to a truck sitting in the middle of a downed portion of the fence.

"Mannie, buzz them. Sometimes, I wish we had guns on this thing," He muttered under his breath.

She looked at him and frowned. "What would you do with guns except get into trouble? You can't shoot them."

Roark sat back. "You're right, we can't, but we can radio the sheriff and tell him where these people are and what the truck looks like. They need a second truck for the four-wheelers. Jubal, get the sheriff's office on the radio."

"That's true. Or they're stashing the animals close

by." She kept her eyes peeled on the ground. "Oh, my God, they're going to shoot—"

A bullet hit the door of the helicopter.

* * *

"MANNIE! GET US OUT OF HERE!" Roark shouted as he leaned over her as if to protect her from anymore bullets.

Jessica sat up and put her right hand on her left side. It came away bloody. "They shot me." She closed her eyes.

"Jessica! Don't close your eyes. You will stay awake." Roark used his deepest, most aggressive voice. The one he used when he was dealing for a company to buy.

She opened her eyes. "You don't need to yell at me. I'm awake but my side hurts, Roark. Why did they shoot at us?"

"Because they are thieves and don't want to be caught. They were trying to shoot us down, I'm sure of it." Roark reached over and patted Mannie on the shoulder. "Thank you for saving our lives today. If you hadn't flown like you did, they have shot us down. Thank you, my friend."

Mannie didn't look back, but kept his eyes on the air in front of him. "You're welcome boss. And Jessica, I'm sorry you got hit. I would fly differently if I had known they would shoot at the 'copter."

She closed her eyes tight and gritted her teeth. "It's

not your fault, and I'm very glad right now to be in this helicopter with you flying it."

Jubal picked up the mic from the dashboard. "Sullivan Industries calling Gallatin County sheriff's office. Over."

The radio crackled. "Sheriff's office. What's your emergency? Over."

"We've got rustlers on the northwest side of the Sullivan ranch. They are in progress now and are shooting at us. Over."

Roark put his hand on the top of Jubal's seatback. "Tell them we are going straight to the hospital."

Jubal pushed the button on the mic. "Gallatin County, we have one person shot in the side. We're taking her directly to Bozeman Health. Over."

"The sheriff will meet you there, and we'll send deputies to the Sullivan Ranch. Over."

"Please alert the hospital we are on our way. Over."

"Will do. Over."

"Sullivan Industries, over and out." Jubal put the mic back.

"How long until we get to the hospital?" asked Roark.

"We're about ten minutes out. How's she doing?" Mannie tried to look around the seat but straightened.

Roark placed his palm on her forehead. "Not good. Her color is gray, and she's getting cold." He ran a hand over her other side and down her back, but didn't find another wound where the bullet would have exited her body.

"Put pressure on the wound. Use your shirt," said Jubal.

Roark whipped off the tee shirt he wore and pressed it against the wound. The bleeding seemed to slow. "Why didn't I think of that?"

"Don't beat yourself up, boss. This has all happened so fast." Mannie pushed the throttle forward, and the helicopter sped up. "I've got it pushed as far as I can. We'll get her there. She'll be okay."

"That's right, Roark. She'll pull through this. She's young and strong." Jubal reached back and squeezed Roark's knee.

"I hope you're right. I don't know what I'll do if I lose her. I just found her."

* * *

THE HELICOPTER LANDED on the pad next to the hospital.

A team of nurses and doctors met them, all of them talking at once.

They loaded Jessica on a gurney and rushed to the ER.

A nurse came by with a clipboard. "Mr. Sullivan?"

"Yes, I'm Roark Sullivan." He stood there, bare chested, and watched as Jessica disappeared inside. "You'll have to talk while we walk."

"We're taking good care of her. Can you tell me what happened?"

"While we were flying over some rustlers on my

ranch, they fired on us, and they hit her. I think it must have been a large caliber bullet since it came from the people on the ground and went through the body of the helicopter."

"Did the bullet exit her body?"

"No."

The nurse jotted down what he said as she jogged alongside him.

He reached the ER entrance and turned to the nurse. "Please find out where she is."

The woman put her clipboard in her left hand and placed her right one on his arm. "She's getting the best of care. I'll find out where she is, and I'll get you a scrub shirt." She turned and left.

He paced the waiting area like a large, predatory cat.

Jubal entered and walked up to him. "Mannie has to move our helicopter so the pad is open for the hospital 'copter."

Roark nodded, but didn't speak or stop pacing.

Jubal paced with him for a few rounds and then found a chair.

They were the only ones in the room now. It was early in the day and he thought the hospital probably got busy after dark.

The nurse came back into the room. "Mr. Sullivan. Here is your shirt, and I have her location now."

"Where is she?" He turned at her voice, took the shirt and slipped it over his head.

"They are just taking her to surgery. Apparently, the

bullet is lodged in her side. You can go wait in the surgical waiting room. The doctor will come out there to talk to you. I have to ask. Are you related to the young woman?"

"She's my fiancée." He lied through his teeth, but if she said yes, then she really would be his fiancée and then his wife. No long engagements this time. A Justice of the Peace would get them legally married, and then she could plan a big to-do if she wanted one. He wasn't letting her get away.

"Okay. The waiting room is on the second floor. Just take those elevators up." She pointed out of the waiting room to the bank of elevators. Both of you can go. I just needed to know who will make decisions, should that become necessary." She shook her head. "Though it's not likely."

"Thank you and thanks for the shirt, too." Roark's strides were long as he reached the elevators and pressed the *up* button. And pressed it again. And again.

Jubal placed a hand on his arm. "That's not going to help it get here any sooner."

Huffing out a breath, he folded his hands together behind his back. "I know."

The elevator arrived just as Mannie came running up. "Glad I didn't miss you. How is she?"

"In surgery. If I find the person who did this, I will make them rue the day they were born."

Was it his imagination, or did Mannie pale? "Tell me what you know, Mannie, or I just might tear you apart right here."

Mannie nodded. "You were right. Alice has been getting messages to the rustlers. I found a burner phone in her purse while she was in the shower. I guess it's been long enough, she thought she had me wrapped around her finger." He fisted his hands. "But if I'd known this would happen…"

Roark set a hand on his friend's shoulder. "Forgive me for my outburst. It's not your fault. It's mine. I'm the one who should have put my foot down."

Jubal laughed. "You'll never be able to," he used finger quotes, "*put your foot down* with that one. She'll run you in circles trying to catch her. And since when is she your fiancée?"

Running a hand behind his neck, he slowly exhaled and then nodded. "Since I just said she was. And you're right, she'll try. She won't succeed and we'll probably fight about it." Then he smiled. "But making up will be great."

Two and a half hours later, a doctor entered the waiting area. He wore green scrubs, with a scrub hat and black Crocs. "Mr. Sullivan?"

Roark's head shot up and he hurried to the doctor. "I'm Roark Sullivan. How is she?"

"She'll be fine. I'm pleased to meet you, Mr. Sullivan." He extended his hand. "I've been to many of your hospital fundraisers. I'm Nick Lowery, the chief of surgery." He released Roark's hand and put it in his scrub pants pocket. "She lost some blood, but the bullet didn't break any bones. She'll be sore and probably shouldn't do any traveling for a week. She also can't lift over five pounds.

"We'll keep her overnight, and then, when we send her home, she should be up and about a couple of hours a day. During those times, she should only do light things. Reading, watching TV—things that don't require a lot of energy for the first week. Then I want her in my office in ten days so I can take out the stitches. She can't shower for a couple of days, and then only if she covers the wound with plastic wrap to keep the bandage dry. Change the bandage in two days and every two days after that. I'll have my nurse give you written instructions to take with you."

Roark extended a hand. "Thank you, Doctor. When can I see her?"

The doctor took his hand. "She's in recovery now. When the nurses are sure she's alert and knows who she is, they'll let you go see her." He lifted a brow. "Last I heard, she was telling them her name was Jessica Sullivan, and you were her husband."

Feeling his face heat, Roark knew his face was flushed. "Not quite yet. But hopefully soon."

The doctor cleared his throat. "I want to thank you for your generosity to the hospital."

"Doctor, if she pulls through, it was worth every penny."

The man smiled. "Then I've done my job. She'll be fine."

The door behind the doctor opened.

A nurse in surgical scrubs, just like the doctor's,

walked up to them. "Doctor, she's alert now and asking for her husband."

"That's me. Where is she?"

The nurse had bright-red hair pulled into a messy ponytail. "Follow me. I'll take you to her."

Roark followed her through an automatic door, down an aisle with rooms formed only by curtains on one side and gurneys and wheelchairs on the other side. He made a left at the end of the aisle and started down another aisle that also had the curtained rooms. But opposite them was the nurses' station, bathroom, and hallways leading off to what he thought were probably operating rooms.

About halfway down this aisle, the nurse came to a halt. "Here we are." She pulled back the curtain.

Roark saw Jessica in a bed. She was very pale and wore a hospital gown.

He walked to her right side and took her hand in his. "How are you feeling, sweetheart?"

She looked up and gave him a wan smile. "I've definitely felt better."

"The doctor said you'll be fine, but no traveling for at least two weeks. I'm afraid you're stuck with me." He squeezed her hand. "And I'm afraid we won't be going camping after all."

"Now, that's really not fair. I get shot and can't go fishing, either." She pouted.

He chuckled. "I'm glad you still have your sense of humor."

"I'm still hopped up on anesthesia and not feeling

any pain. What will you do with me for two weeks while I recover? I have to call my mom. We have our regular dinner date on Sunday. How am I supposed to explain why I was shot?"

His mouth formed a flat line, and he shrugged. "I've never been very good at dealing with family problems. That's what my mother is for."

"Your poor mother."

Frowning, he slowly shook his head. "It's true. She's so put-upon." He grinned. "She loves it. We make her feel useful. That's not to say she isn't already, but some-times..." He shrugged.

She smiled, and her eyes were narrowed. "I know. My mother worries about me, too. Which reminds me, I was teasing before. We cannot, under any circum-stances, tell her they shot me. She will absolutely lose her mind."

"We wouldn't want that. The doctor wants to keep you overnight. I'm staying if they will let me."

"You don't need to. I'll be sleeping most of the time anyway, and I don't want to worry about you."

"You don't need to worry about me. I am just watching over you. I'm your own guardian angel."

"I don't need a guardian angel."

"I'm protecting my fiancée, at least I hope my fiancée. Jessica, please marry me. I don't know how to tell you how I feel. I've been trying, but you don't seem to understand or want to understand, so I'll come right out and say it. I love you. Marry me. Anytime you want, I'll be here, waiting for you. Waiting for your answer.

JESSICA TOUCHED her lips with the fingertips of her right hand. *He wants to marry me. Isn't that really what I've hoped for all along? So why am I holding back? He says he loves me. But how can he really know in such a short amount of time?*

Why do I question his feelings when I feel the same way? I love him. But how can that be? If don't I trust my own feelings, how can I trust his?

CHAPTER 12

he next day, the doctor released Jessica to go home. Roark entered the room and found Jessica standing and leaning on the bed. He hurried to support her before she collapsed. "What are you doing? You should have waited for me."

She whispered. "Regardless of what I told them, we aren't really engaged, and I didn't want you to see me."

He whispered in her ear. "We aren't engaged because I've been trying to give you time. The fact we haven't known each other for some arbitrary length of time you seem to feel we need before we can get married isn't my idea. I want to marry you, now, today, every day."

Her legs seemed to give way.

He held her against him until she could stand on her own. Quietly, he said against her cheek. "Don't answer me now, sweetheart. Let me help you get dressed, and we'll worry about wedding dates after you're well. And I promise to stay behind you to give you your modesty."

She nodded.

Jessica was embarrassed the entire time Roark helped her. He had her sit in the plastic chair they always have in the hospital rooms while he put her shoes on for her.

"There we go. Let me get an orderly. They have to wheel you outside and I have to get Jubal and Mannie." He leaned down and did what he'd been dying to do since he first saw her in the recovery room. He kissed her and tried to put all his love for her into the kiss.

Finally, he pulled back. "Tell me you didn't feel what I did, because if you do, then you're a liar, which I know you're not." He gave her a quick peck and walked out of the room.

He met her outside with a paper in his hand. He held it up. "Instructions for your home care. This way, I don't have to remember it all."

They pushed Jessica in a wheelchair all the way out to the helicopter. Thankfully, the flight home in the helicopter was uneventful. Roark kept hold of her hand, like he was afraid she'd disappear if he let go.

When they landed back at his ranch, he refused to let her walk to the house and carried her the entire way. He wasn't even winded when they arrived in the kitchen, and he finally let her down.

Even though she felt a jolt of pain, she did her best not to let it show and looked up at him and smiled. "It was very nice of you to carry me, but I could have walked. I would have been slow, but I would have made it."

"You can't use those crutches with that wound on your side. You either start walking on your ankle, which I don't recommend, or you let me carry you, which I would prefer to do."

"Well, you must let me walk around the house. I'm not the type of person who can just sit around, but if I have to, I suppose I could read. I can also write. That doesn't take a lot of physical strength."

"What I want for you to do now is rest, like the doctor said. You are supposed to rest and do light things like read and watch TV."

She rolled her eyes, then realized she *was* tired, and she hadn't even done anything yet. "I suppose you're right. I am tired. Getting shot seems to have taken all my strength."

He smiled and tilted his head a little. "You also had surgery, so twice the trauma." He bent and picked her up again. "I'll see if Athena has any broth. According to the printed instructions the nurse gave me, you should probably go easy with solid food until you're sure you can keep it down. In the meantime, you're going to bed; your actual bed, not the sofa in the den." He carried her up to the guest room and set her down on the left side of the bed. "Do you have pajamas or a nightgown?"

"In the second drawer of the dresser."

He retrieved the garment and returned to her by

the bed. "Let's get you out of those clothes and into bed."

"I'm too tired to argue with you."

He gazed down at her. "Would you rather I get Athena?"

She looked up at him. "Yes, I would. I have nothing to hide, but we're not married, and I'd prefer we didn't get too personal...in case we don't."

He cupped her face. "Sweetheart, we will be married. And as far as I'm concerned, the sooner, the better." He dropped to one knee. "Jessica Kirby, will you do me the honor of becoming my wife?"

She looked down into his beloved face. "Yes, I will." Her heart pounded, and she was suddenly moved to tears. They filled her eyes, but they were happy tears.

He rose and took her into his arms. "I love you Jessica Kirby. I've known it from the moment our hands first touched. You're special. You're the only woman I ever want to be with, Mrs. Sullivan."

She noticed the soft pressure as he was careful of her bandages. She wrapped her right arm around his neck, even though the action made her left side ache. "I love you, too. I didn't want to admit it. It's so sudden, but I felt the same way when we touched the first time. Electricity shot through me. It...it was like nothing I've ever felt before. I still get a little jolt when we touch. Do you?"

"I do." He kissed her.

"Poor Mannie, I think he might have actually liked her."

Roark didn't look sorry for his employee and friend. "Maybe, but he knew from the beginning not to get involved. We suspected she was in the gang stealing the cattle. Until she got involved with Mannie, we didn't know how they were getting the information on where to hit. It was never the same place twice."

"And Mannie found out by being with Alice?" She slumped onto the bed. Her body was exhausted. She needed to be in her nightgown and in bed. She needed to rest. No reading or writing today.

"He did. He'd given her a burner phone, but he found another in her purse and gave me the number. My team in Bozeman tracked the phone and transcribed all the calls and texts. The man behind it all is another rancher, named Kevin Nelson. His ranch is south of mine. We were waiting for him to make this last move. He told Alice this was it—his last haul. He had enough cattle now. He needs to rebrand them and thinks they'll be his."

She heard the satisfaction in his voice. "Thinks? What am I missing? Wait, before you tell me, help me into my nightgown. I can't wait for you to get Athena. I want to get into bed now."

"All right. I'll be the soul of discretion and not look…again."

"Thank you."

Roark helped her out of her clothes from behind, and when she was down to her underwear, he pulled the soft silk nightgown over her head.

"This is a very nice gown. Did you plan on wearing it just for me?"

"Yes," she looked over her shoulder. "But don't get a big head. I wanted to look pretty." She was embarrassed to admit she was dressing for him. "I have a robe that goes with it, so I would be quite modest."

"Well, Miss Modest, get into bed, and I'll tuck you in."

"I am tired. For some reason, I feel like someone shot me."

Roark chuckled. "Enough. You'll start laughing, and then I'll be in trouble." He turned down the bedsheets.

She got between the sheets and winced in pain.

He tucked them around her, careful of her left side, and then sat on the bed next to her.

Now that she was in bed and relaxed, she wanted to know more. "Okay, tell me about the cattle and Kevin Nelson."

"We have someone on the inside at his ranch. He said Kevin's already rebranding the stolen cattle. He's taken pictures of the process and of Kevin doing part of it himself." He shook his head. "Why he is doing the branding himself, I don't know. The owner of the cows is supposed to be the last one to brand them—to put the final brand on himself. His signature, so to speak and maybe by following the accustomed procedure for branding, he thinks it makes it almost legal. At least legal enough for him."

"And you have a picture showing him applying the new one over the old one?"

"We do. Now, I just have to pull my man out of there, but I can't until the sheriff has Nelson and my man in jail." Roark turned and paced away from the bed and then back again. His mouth was in a thin line and he clenched his jaw. "He'll arrest them both, and then it doesn't matter if Nelson knows who he is or not. Until then, his life is in danger. If Nelson finds out about him before we can extract him, his life would be forfeit."

Her eyes widened and then narrowed. "He'll kill him? But right now he's only rustling cattle. He hasn't killed anyone. He'll go to prison forever if he commits murder."

"I know. I don't want my man killed, which is why I need to extract him. Now."

"How do you plan on doing that so Nelson doesn't kill him or escape?"

"It will be a joint operation with the sheriff's department. They will make the raid on the Nelson ranch, as they are branding the cattle." He looked down at his watch. "That should happen now. Johnny will be arrested, too, along with every man out there. I'm hoping there aren't many. I don't need everyone to know he was my man. Nelson isn't the only rustler, just the biggest one, and Johnny might come in handy to take down the other rustlers."

Jessica frowned. "I think you're playing with that man's life. Even if he isn't arrested with the rest of the gang, his allegiance will get out. Secrets always do."

He furrowed his brows and pursed his lips, chewing on the inside of one cheek.

Jessica almost smiled. He looked like he had a lopsided pucker, but there was nothing to smile about. "Johnny is in serious danger. If those rustlers would shoot at your helicopter when they had to know who it belonged to, they wouldn't think twice about killing someone they saw as a traitor."

"I'll talk to the sheriff. You might be right. I want to communicate with Johnny, too. It's his life we're putting in danger, after all."

She rolled her eyes. If she didn't hurt so much, she'd get out of that bed and punch Roark to get his attention. "Of course, he'll say yes. He wants to impress you, since you're his boss." She narrowed her eyes. "But that's what you're counting on, isn't it?" She put a hand on his arm. "Please, Roark, don't do this. Thank him for his work, give him a raise and a horse, and let him be a cowboy again."

Roark crossed his arms over his chest. "I love you, but do you really think I would put my man at risk forever? Do you think I'm that callous? Besides, I think the sheriff has his own ideas about the other rustlers. He might make a deal with Nelson. We'll see."

"I really wish I wasn't in this bed. I'd punch you."

"I don't enjoy fighting with you. I'll go see if Athena has any broth." He lowered his head until he felt her lips beneath his and he kissed her. Then he turned toward the door.

When he returned, he had a bed tray with the broth,

crackers, and a glass of milk. "Just eat what you want. Don't feel you have to finish anything. It's a lot of food for your tummy right now."

He bent over and slowly, gently kissed her. This was a lover's kiss, not carnal, but full of love. She felt it to her very toes. When she felt him pulling away, she followed him, unwilling to let the kiss end. "With a kiss like that, I'd say we should get married as soon as possible."

Roark smiled. "We'll get a marriage license when you're well and then we can get married whenever we want, up to one-hundred and eighty days from when we get it."

She lifted a brow and crossed her arms over the blankets covering her chest, making her stitches pull. She lowered her left arm back to the bed. "You know an awful lot about getting married in Montana."

He grinned and waggled his brows. "I looked it up as soon as I knew you were coming. I wanted to be prepared."

She laughed, then winced. "Oh, oh. That hurts. Don't make me laugh. Please. I beg of you."

"Honey, I don't do it on purpose. For some reason, you just find me funny. I don't know whether to be pleased or insulted."

She waved her right hand. "Pleased. My mother said if you can laugh once every day when you're married, you'll have a happy marriage. That's not to say we won't have arguments, I'm sure we will. We're both...

independent people. There's something I want you to know."

"What is it?"

He looked scared. His brows lifted a little in the middle, and his eyes narrowed slightly. He tilted his head just a smidge.

"It's not bad news. I just want you to know I'm not marrying you for your money. I make enough money to live comfortably. I'm actually quite a successful author."

His head jerked back liked he'd been slapped. "But you write romance novels."

She sighed. "If I didn't get this response from just about everyone, I'd be insulted. Romance novels are the highest earning genre of fiction and are thirty-three percent of all books sold in mass market paperback."

He raised his hands, palms out. "I didn't mean to offend."

"You didn't. Most people operate under the same prejudices that you do. Women who are lacking a love life are the only ones who read romance novels, or they are old or not well educated, or they have any number of other prejudices. All of which are untrue. But I'm not about to tell you all the numbers when you can look them up for yourself, and I'm too tired to argue."

"You need to get some rest."

"Lie with me until I go to sleep. Please?"

He raised his eyebrows and then relaxed them and smiled. "I'd love to lie down with you." Roark took off his shoes and laid on her left side so her injury was between them and he was less likely to hurt her by accident. He placed an arm over the top of her pillow so she could cuddle into his side. Then, when she had, he brought his arm down and around her.

She sniffed. "Mmm. You smell good. This is nice. Why can't we always be like this? Why do we have to fight?"

ROARK STOOD and looked down at the woman he was about to marry. Dark lashes lay against her pale, too pale, skin. She'd lost all color, and he worried about her.

He'd check her wound every day, and if she was feeling particularly modest, he'd have Athena check on her.

He brought one of the Queen Anne chairs from his room next to her bed, grabbed a book—one of her novels—belonging to Athena, and got comfortable.

She was on her right side, then turned onto her back and moaned, but didn't wake.

Athena came in with a small thermal pot of coffee and a cup. "Thought you might need this."

"Thanks. I do." He looked up at her. "Do we have a thermometer that you don't have to touch her to take her temperature?"

"We do. I'll get it and be right back." She left and returned a few minutes later with what looked like a ray gun. "Here you go. Just aim it at her forehead from about six inches away."

He did. The reading was 101 degrees. She had a low grade temperature. "I think she's got an infection. Call the doctor while I get the bandages off." He stopped. "Wait. She's very modest. You take her clothes off and remove the bandages so we can look at the wound. I think we have enough stuff here to redo her bandages, but if not, we'll send someone to get some more. I'll call the doctor."

"That would be me, since I know what to look for and the men don't."

He looked up at his housekeeper and friend, more grateful than ever for her. "Thanks, Athena."

She waved him off. "You'd do the same for me."

"I would."

She set a hand on his shoulder. "I know, and that's why I'm still here after all these years. Jubal feels the same way."

He covered her hand with his where it lay on his shoulder. "Thank you."

"Of course." She removed her hand. "Now, let's get her bandage open and see what's going on."

When Athena got the bandages off, Roark looked at the wounds. They both were oozing small amounts of yellow discharge.

He turned his gaze toward Athena. "The doctor said if we see yellow discharge we are supposed to call her back and she will prescribe some antibiotics."

"We better get some, then. The sooner she takes them, the sooner the infection will go away."

"I'll call her back. Would you clean the wound while I do? Then I'll help you re-bandage her."

An hour later, between him and Athena, they had cleaned her wound, changed Jessica's bandage, redressed her and gotten her back into bed.

"I hate the fact that she's gotten an infection. I'll call the pharmacy and make sure they got the prescription for the antibiotics."

"Good. I need to start dinner. Let me know if anything changes."

"I will."

Roark paid the pharmacist's son to drive the prescription of antibiotics out to the ranch.

Just a couple of hours later, Jessica was awake and driving everyone crazy with her requests.

Finally, the next day, she told everyone she was sorry for yesterday and got around the house on one crutch.

She walked down to the kitchen. "Hello, Athena. I want to apologize. I know I'm a terrible patient. Thank you for all you've done."

Athena smiled. "Roark did most of it. He was the only one you'd listen to."

"Oh, no wonder he doesn't want to be around me anymore. Did he tell you he wants to marry me? I said yes." Her stomach was upset and she couldn't eat. "I wonder if he'll take back his proposal?"

CHAPTER 13

"No, he's not about to take back his proposal."

Jessica swung around at the sound of Roark's deep baritone behind her. "Ouch. I didn't hear you come in."

"So I surmised." He walked close and took her in his arms, careful of her injury. "The fact you wouldn't do anything for anyone but me only convinced me you love me. I didn't leave to get away, but to get you this." He stepped back and went down on one knee. "Jessica, I love you with all my heart. Will you still marry me?" He held out a beautiful ring with a large oval cut diamond in the center surrounded by dark blue sapphires. "It was my grandmother's engagement ring. I got it from the house when we went there to get the convertible."

Tears of joy ran down her cheeks, and she didn't even try to brush them away. "I'll still marry you."

He placed the ring on her finger. It fit like it was

made specially for her. "That is just another sign, if you believe in that kind of thing, that you are the perfect woman for me. I've never wanted to give this ring ffffffto any other woman." Roark stood and took her face between his palms and kissed her.

It was slow, like he was learning her lips and her mouth for the first time.

He pulled away.

"I want to get a license as soon as you're able and get married as soon as we can after that. Later, if you want, we can do the whole big wedding. Does that work for you? I've asked Judge Stone to work us in when you're ready."

"Perfect. Let's go tomorrow. I'm feeling pretty good and if we don't stay out for too long, I should make it."

"Whether or not you feel good, the doctor wanted you to rest for a week. And it would behoove us to wait until you get your stitches out. Then we can make a day of it—stitches—license—marriage ceremony and then home for our wedding night." He lowered his voice and ran a finger from her temple down her jawline to her neck and then down her neck to her shoulder. Then he slid his hand around the back of her neck and brought her close. "I can't wait to make love to you."

She shivered with need. Her heart pounded, and she was sure Roark could hear it. "I want that too, very much…and you're right, the night will be much better for both of us if we don't have to worry about my injury."

"Good, now why don't you go back upstairs and get into bed? I want you to be as much back to normal as possible in ten days...when you get your stitches out. Did Athena tell you..." He looked around the room. "Where did she go?"

"Probably out, so we'd have some privacy."

"You're right. Let's let her back into her kitchen. She has many people to cook for. This is pork roast night. The boys tire of beef, but when you live on a cattle ranch, you eat beef."

"I hadn't thought about it. I'm a meat eater, so it's been fine, though I do love pork, too."

"You truly are a woman after mine own heart."

She grinned. "I'm not after your heart anymore...I have it, just as you have mine. Now, let's go upstairs. You can put me to bed, and we can talk about our wedding. Since we're waiting for ten days, I'm sure our parents can be here by then, and we won't have to have two weddings. Just the one before Judge Stone."

His eyebrows slashed down. "You don't still want the white wedding dress and the church and big champagne reception? You'll do without all of that?"

Jessica set the pace for walking back up to her bedroom. It was slow, but she could put a little more weight on her ankle, but she still needed the crutch. "As long as you're beside me, I don't need anything else. There are only two people I want here. My mom and my best friend Lanie. She'll be my maid of honor."

"I don't know which of my brothers I'll ask to be my best man. Whoever I choose, I will hurt the other."

"Does it have to be one of your brothers? What about your best friend? Trevor, wasn't it?"

"That's a good idea. Then no one gets their feelings hurt."

"They can all come up in your plane. There's plenty of room, but what about after they arrive? We don't have enough room for them. We have the two spare rooms for our parents…but—"

"Shh. My parents and brothers have their own homes here on the ranch. We'll put your mother and Lanie up here in our spare rooms. After the ceremony, we'll have an extra room, anyway." He waggled his eyebrows.

She laughed then clutched her side. "Stop. Please. Oww. Oww. Don't make me laugh. Please, I'm begging you. What about Trevor? Where will he stay?"

Roark took her hand. "Sweetheart, I'm sorry for making you laugh. You're always a wonderful audience, but I need to remember your injury. Trevor will stay with James and his family. They're good friends, too. I met Trevor through James. It's a long story which I'll tell you sometime."

They reached her bedroom and walked inside.

"I'm definitely not up to snuff. That little bit of exercise has worn me out. I have to go to bed now and sleep."

"I told you the doctor wanted you to rest. We both need to adhere to that advice. You won't have a problem going to sleep. You are white as a sheet and have dark circles under your eyes. A good long nap will take care of both."

"If you say so. Will you help me take this robe off? I suddenly don't seem to have the energy or the dexterity to do it."

He slid the robe off her right arm and then let the silk fall down her left arm. She was thankful he didn't hit her wound, since she didn't think she could handle him even lightly touching her injury right now. "Roark, thank you for taking care of the infection. I hope it will stay away for the rest of my ten days."

"Me, too, sweetheart. Me, too."

THE FAMILIES ARRIVED on day nine of Jessica's confinement. She was feeling fantastic and very ready to have her stitches out and to get married. She asked her mother to bring the red dress Roark had purchased for her for the gala and her black patent four-inch heels. When she'd asked Roark if the gems on the bodice of the dress were real, he confirmed they were. She'd taken a deep breath and decided she really needed a large safe deposit box. She couldn't have a dress that expensive just hanging in her loft. But she'd decided the dress was good luck because it brought her and Roark closer. Without the dress, she wouldn't have gone to the dance, just the auction, like she always did.

Three black SUVs pulled into the drive in front of the house.

Jessica saw them from her bedroom window and practically skipped down the stairs. She had so much to tell her mother and Lanie. She threw the door open and ran across the porch and down the steps.

Her mother and Lanie were in the first Tahoe with Roark's parents, who she knew from pictures in the house. His father was driving. *They must leave the vehicles at the airport for when they need them.*

"Mom!" She almost tackled her mother; she was so happy to see her. She wrapped her in a bear hug.

"Jessi. How are you? You know, it's only been about three weeks since we saw each other, but it seems like forever. What's going on?" Sally Kirby put her daughter at arm's length and searched her face. "You've changed. You're really in love, aren't you?"

"I am. More than I ever thought possible." She turned to Lanie. "Hi, my friend. I'm so glad you could come on such short notice. You will be my maid of honor, won't you? You can't say no...you're my best friend."

Lanie grinned. "Do you think I'd come all this way just to say no?"

Jessica laughed and shook her head. "I don't suppose you would." She stepped back. "Come on in. We've got iced tea," she looked over at her mother, "unsweetened tea and a light snack in the living room. Follow me."

When they reached the living room, Roark joined them.

He went first to Sally and took her right hand in

his. "Mrs. Kirby, will you grant me the honor of marrying your daughter? I promise I'll take good care of her, and I'll love her always to the best of my ability."

Sally covered their clasped hands with her left one. "I would love to welcome you into the family, Roark Sullivan. I've never seen my daughter so happy, but you have to promise me something else."

His eyes narrowed and his eyebrows formed black slashes over his eyes. "What? I'll do anything."

"Don't let her get shot again. I don't think my heart could take it. Though I am glad you decided to tell me. I appreciate being kept informed of my daughter's health."

Roark smiled down at her mother. "I promise I will do my best, but she can be a stubborn woman, and certainly not one I would ever attempt to control."

Her mom pulled her hands free and then wrapped her arms around Roark, who was a good eight inches taller. "You'll do. Thank you for loving my girl and making her so happy."

Roark hugged her back and then turned toward the group of people behind him, waiting to sit. "Everyone, take a seat, and we'll answer your questions." He took Jessica's hand and sat on one of the sofas.

Surprisingly, their families didn't have any questions. They'd discussed everything between them on the plane trip to Bozeman.

"We want to know when the wedding is, exactly," said Marian Sullivan. Her silver hair was cut in a very becoming short bob. She was about Jessica's height and weight. "Sally, Lanie and I discussed it on the plane ride here. We need time to prepare, and I'm sure Jessica will, too."

"I intend to dress before we leave to get my stitches out tomorrow. Then we'll get the license and from there proceed immediately to Judge Stone's court and get married. He already knows we're coming and has said he'd be willing to stop whatever he's doing for us. Isn't that sweet?" Jessica leaned into Roark's side. "After the wedding, we'll have a meal...lunch or dinner, but probably a very late lunch."

Roark squeezed her hand. "I'm sure it will be fine. Tomorrow is Thursday, and unless everyone is getting ready for a weekend wedding, we should be okay."

Jessica brought his hand to her lips and kissed the back. "It'll be September 21st and there aren't any holidays around that time that I can think of." She suddenly jumped in her seat. "Mom, Lanie, I forgot to show you my engagement ring." She held up her hand and wiggled her fingers. The large diamond sparkled in the light.

Lanie, who sat in the chair at the left end of the sofa, sucked in a breath. "Oh, my gosh, that's gorgeous."

Jessica looked over at Roark's mother. "Mrs. Sullivan, thank you for letting him have it for me."

"You must call me Marian." She put her hand to her chest. "He's never asked for it before. Not with all six of his engagements, he never once asked for his grandmother's ring. I knew those women wouldn't last, and he wouldn't marry any one of them. But when I met you and saw him with you, I knew. And he confirmed it when he asked for the ring."

Jessica felt her cheeks heat and knew she blushed. She wrapped her arms around Roark's arm and leaned into his body. "I didn't even know it then. I should have known by his touch, but I was still trying to deny what was happening. Even though I must have known and must have believed it, because I agreed to come here with him after knowing him for only two days." She looked up at him. "I'd never even gone on a second date with anyone in just two days."

He pulled his arm free and put it around her shoulders, then brought her closer. "I'd never brought anyone here before, but I couldn't imagine coming here without her."

Trevor rolled his blue eyes. His blond hair was just below his ears, and he flicked it out of his eyes with a shake of his head. "Boy, you two have it bad. What I want to know is if Miss Lanie would like to go for a walk. Would you?" He made his way to the front door and held out his arm.

Lanie blushed and dipped her chin. "Yes, I would like that." She stood and walked around the sofa to take his arm. "Where are we going?"

"Wherever you'd like, pretty lady."

Lanie looked back at Jessica with a twinkle in her dark brown eyes. "A silver tongue this one has. Will my honor be safe?"

Jessica laughed and then shrugged. "You know him better than I do. We only met at the gala before today and that wasn't a happy time. You just spent three hours with him. But I have a feeling you will both need to worry about your honor."

Lanie threw back her head and laughed, tossing her long black hair that hung in loose curls to the middle of her back. She'd removed the cornrows and the braid, opting to let her hair be loose and natural. She took Trevor's arm, and the two disappeared out the front door.

"How about we let you all unpack, and we'll meet back here around six o'clock for dinner?" asked Roark.

"That sounds good, son." Marian Sullivan stood.

Her husband, Riley, stood, too. He walked over to Roark and Jessica. He was nearly as tall as Roark. His hair was still dark, and he had silver streaks on the sides, just like Roark. "I'm so glad you finally found each other, and I'm glad you're not playing games. Your mother and I married after knowing each other for only a week. Everyone, all of our families and friends, told us we were crazy. That was forty-two years ago, and I still know she's the only woman for me."

Jessica watched Riley as he gazed at his wife. She was warm inside seeing such love and pride like she'd seen on the face of only one other man...her father... when he looked at her mother. Would Roark look at her like that someday?

CHAPTER 14

The next morning, Jessica was up and showered by six a.m. She finger-combed her hair, then put on her robe and went to Lanie's room. She knocked on the door, waited, and then knocked again.

The door slowly opened. Lanie had her robe on and her hair was still beautiful. It would be called 'bedhead' today and was very much in style.

"What?"

Jessica pushed her way inside. "I need a blow dryer. Did you bring yours?"

"No, I didn't bring mine. I don't need it. You could always let your hair go natural, and we'd be twins." She laughed as she headed back to the bedroom. "Well, except for the fact I'm black and you're not."

"No one will pay any attention to that. Did mother give you the dress I told her to bring?"

Lanie rolled her eyes. "I can hear. Of course, I brought it."

Jessica hugged her friend. "That peach color is so gorgeous on you and that dress is beautiful. We'll be the best-dressed women at the doctor's office and the courthouse."

"Are you going to ask your mother for a hair dryer?"

She shook her head. "I'm taking your advice and wearing it au naturel."

Lanie yawned and leaned against the doorjamb to the bedroom. "Good, now, can I go back to sleep?"

Jessica grinned, walked to her friend, and put her arms around her before giving her a big, noisy kiss on the cheek. "Yes, you can sleep for another hour and then you have to be up doing my makeup. I want it to be very special. After all, it's my wedding day."

She rolled her eyes and wiped her cheek with her palm. "Fine. Goodnight."

Jessica shook her head and laughed. "Goodnight. See you in an hour." She practically floated back to her room.

Two hours later, she was in her beautiful red dress and patent leather heels. Her makeup was perfect, and her hair was in loose curls down her back.

Roark stood at the bottom of the stairs, looking up.

The small smile that crossed his face was just for her. His eyes focused only on her.

She reached the last stair.

He held out his arm.

She took his arm and descended to stand beside him. Looking around the room, she saw nothing but smiling faces. "Are we ready to do this? The doctor's office opened at eight."

Roark patted her hand where it lay on his arm. "Don't worry. It'll all be good."

Butterflies filled her stomach, and she felt nauseous. She knew better than to eat now. "I'm just nervous."

He bent and whispered in her ear, "You look beautiful, but I can't wait to take that dress off…and not turn my back, but to see you in all your glory."

She laughed. "All right, folks, I'm ready. My dear, nearly husband has come to the rescue and kept me from vomiting from nerves."

"Let's get going. Are you all sure you want to go to the doctor with us? You can go to the courthouse and wait. We shouldn't be long. The doctor's office is just a couple of blocks from there." Roark moved toward the door.

"I think that's a good idea," said Trevor.

Jessica saw everyone else give their nod of approval.

"Let's go, then." Roark headed out the door.

Jessica took his arm again once they were outside. She placed her right hand over her left as it circled the crook of his elbow. *Am I making a mistake? Is a love like I've never known before enough to build a happy marriage?*

AT THE DOCTOR'S OFFICE, the nurse showed Jessica into a room. The doctor entered a couple of minutes later. He grinned when he saw her.

"Hi, Jessica. I think you're a little overdressed for this visit. How are you?"

"I'm ready to get these stitches out. Roark and I are going to the courthouse to get our marriage license after we leave here." She waved her hand up and down the front of her body. "That's why I'm dressed this way. This is the dress I wore for our first date, and I figure it's good luck."

Doctor Lowery laughed. "I guess you must be right. I understand you're the first woman he's brought to Bozeman."

She gasped. "How would you know that?"

"It's not a huge city. My nurse told me. Her husband told her, and he has a friend who has a friend, who has a friend who works at the Sullivan ranch. Now, shall we remove those stitches so you can get married?"

"Oh, yes, please." She unzipped her dress and dropped the top so the doctor could get to her wound.

He moved over to the table and looked at her wound. "This looks great. I'd say you, or your nurses, did a fantastic job."

She stared at one of those human circulatory system posters on the wall in front of her. "Thanks. I had one bout with infection, but you know that."

"I do." He picked up his scissors and snipped the stitches, then used tweezers to remove them. "There you go. All done."

She pulled her dress up. "Doctor Lowery, would you zip me up, please?"

"Of course." He moved behind her and zipped her up.

"Thanks, Doctor. I appreciate all you did today very much. Excuse me if I don't stay."

He scooted her out with a motion of his hands. "Of course. Go. I'll check you out with my nurse."

"Thank you." She hurried out to the waiting room, where Roark paced. "I'm ready." She smiled. "Are you?"

He walked over to her, then leaned down and kissed her lightly. "I am. I've never been more ready for anything in my life."

She widened her eyes. "You know this is a life sentence you're undertaking. There is no going back. I don't believe in divorce." *I probably should have brought this subject up before now. What if he says he definitely believes in divorce?*

"I don't either." He held out a hand. "Let's go."

She let out the breath she'd been holding. Then she lifted her skirt and walked out of the office, to the parking lot and Roark's dark blue Yukon.

He drove the two blocks to the courthouse and met the rest of their party in the Gallatin County Clerk and Recorder's office.

They were the third in line for help. When it was their turn, they walked up to the counter.

The woman there smiled. "Let me guess. You two would like a marriage license, is that right?"

Jessica grinned and then looked up at Roark.

He smiled back and then turned toward the woman. "Yes, ma'am, that is correct. Then we're going to Judge Stone's courtroom and getting married."

"Well, let's get this done, then."

They filled out the application. The clerk approved it and issued the license.

"Thank you so much." Jessica lifted her skirt and walked with Roark, followed by their family and friends, to Judge Stone's courtroom.

The judge was in his sixties with a balding head and glasses. Sitting behind his desk on the raised dais, the judge looked up as they came in and smiled. Then he pounded his gavel. "Ladies and gentlemen. We will take a short recess. Please clear the courtroom."

The room, which had not been full by any means, cleared quickly.

"All right Roark, you and Jessica come forward with your witnesses. The rest of you can take a seat."

Roark put out an arm.

Jessica wrapped a shaking hand around the crook of his elbow.

He covered her hand with his and squeezed gently.

She looked up at him and smiled.

"Are you ready?" he whispered.

She nodded. "As ready as I'll ever be."

"Okay. Let's go." Roark moved toward the judge.

The judge walked down the steps from his desk to the courtroom floor, carrying a small book.

Roark and Jessica stopped just in front of him.

Trevor and Lanie followed.

Lanie in the lead.

They took their places just behind Roark and Jessica.

To Roark's right stood Trevor, and to Jessica's left stood Lanie.

Judge Stone opened the book to a marked page and then looked up. "Are you ready to get married?"

"Yes, sir," said Jessica.

"I am, Your Honor," said Roark, extending the license.

"Very well." He looked at the marriage license and then turned toward Roark. "Roark Edward Sullivan, do you take this woman to be your wife, to live together in holy matrimony, to love her, to honor her, to comfort her, and to keep her in sickness and in health, forsaking all others, for as long as you both shall live?"

Roark took her right hand in his. "I do."

"And do you, Jessica Ann Kirby, take this man to be your husband, to live together in holy matrimony, to love him, to honor him, to comfort him, and to keep him in sickness and in health, forsaking all others, for as long as you both shall live?"

She looked up at the man she was marrying. "I do." Her heart filled near to bursting with love.

"Good. Roark repeat after me. I, Roark Edward Sullivan, take you, Jessica Ann Kirby, to be my wife, to have and to hold from this day forward, for better, for worse, for richer, for poorer, in sickness and in health, to love and to cherish, till death do us part."

Roark gazed into her eyes and repeated the words the judge said.

The judge turned toward Jessica. "Repeat after me. I, Jessica Ann Kirby, take you, Roark Edward Sullivan, to be my husband, to have and to hold from this day forward, for better, for worse, for richer, for poorer, in sickness and in health, to love and to cherish, till death do us part."

Jessica repeated the words. She looked into Roark's emerald eyes and knew she was doing the absolutely right thing.

"Are there rings to be exchanged?" asked the judge.

"Yes," said Jessica and Roark together.

He chuckled.

She laughed softly.

"Now, repeat after me," said the judge. "With this ring, I thee wed."

Roark put a wedding band on her finger and then he brought her hand up and kissed the rings.

Lanie handed Jessica a simple gold band.

Roark raised a brow as he looked down and watched her.

"With this ring, I thee wed." Jessica pushed the ring onto his finger. It surprised her to see it was just a little loose.

The judge smiled and brought his hands down in front of him. "By the power vested in me by the State of Montana, county of Gallatin and City of Bozeman, I now pronounce you husband and wife. You may kiss your bride."

Roark cupped her face in his hands and then kissed her slowly, but thoroughly, without delving into the depths of her mouth. When he pulled back, he gazed at her. "I love you."

"And I do you. I never thought I could be so happy." With her pulse racing, she turned to their family and friends and held up her left hand and wiggled her fingers. "We did it." Her voice was breathy, and she needed to rest.

Roark put an arm around her waist. "I've arranged for brunch at the Riverside Country Club." He looked over at Athena. "I want Athena and Jubal to enjoy the day as much as we do."

Roark turned toward the judge. "What do I owe you?"

"One-hundred-dollars, even. I put it in a fund for the children's after-school programs at my grandson's elementary."

"That's great." Roark took two one-hundred-dollar bills from his wallet and handed them to the judge. "There's one from me, too."

The judge lifted the bills and squeezed them. "The kids thank you."

Jessica squeezed Roark's hand. "Are we ready to go?"

He cocked a brown and grinned. "In a hurry, are we?"

She rolled her eyes. "Yes, I'm hungry."

He looked down and whispered. "So am I, but not for food."

She ducked her head and felt the fire in her cheeks. Jessica slapped his chest. "Behave."

Roark grabbed her hand and kissed it. "Never."

She laughed and gazed up at him. "Will we always be this way? Love each other this much?"

He shook his head. "No. We won't. Our love will grow more and more each day, because I can't imagine loving you less than I do now, only more. I'll love you forever, my Jessica."

"As I will you. Forever. Now, let's go eat."

EPILOGUE

 wo years later

JESSICA PADDED AROUND THE BEDROOM, getting dressed in the walk-in closet where she could turn on the light and not wake Roark.

She looked down and rubbed a circle on her belly. "I'm ready to meet you, little one. I don't know who you are yet, but your daddy and I are prepared either way." She put on a bra and pulled a simple A-line dress over her head. Jessica debated whether she should put on underwear, but decided they'd just have to take them off anyway, so why bother?

After she dressed, she picked up the small weekender she'd prepared to take to the hospital.

Jessica looked at her bump again. "I guess we better wake your father. I'm not prepared to drive myself to the hospital." She went into the bedroom and to Roark's side of the bed. He looked so peaceful. His hair was mussed like he'd been doing handstands into his pillow. He still was the most handsome man she'd ever known.

Neither of them would ever sleep like this again once the baby came home. Sleep would be a luxury. But they had talked about this, and Roark insisted he would help. She still didn't know how he would do that since she'd be nursing, but she supposed she could pump so he could feed the baby and bond with him or her.

She shook his shoulder. "Roark, honey, wake up. It's time." She stood back.

Roark popped up like a jack-in-the-box. "Time. It's time to go. Jessica?"

She turned on the lamp on his nightstand. "Yes, dear. It's time to go. My water broke, and my contractions are less than five minutes apart."

"Okay. I'll dress and get the car." He rubbed his eyes and then stood and walked to the closet. He returned in a few minutes in jeans, a western shirt and cowboy boots.

It was his standard wardrobe these days. They'd made their home in Montana at the Sullivan ranch. Now they'd head to the hospital, and their baby would be born…a rancher…girl or boy.

They'd chosen not to know the sex of the child, preferring instead to be surprised, just as their parents had been.

Jessica's mother had traveled to Montana for the birth.

Roark's parents would fly in after the baby was born.

"Roark, I think you should hurry. Owww." She grabbed her belly and rubbed it, bending a little at the waist. Anything to relieve the discomfort.

Roark's eyes widened and his mouth dropped open. "Okay, let's get you downstairs and into the truck. Or do you need to fly? I can have Mannie here in less than ten minutes."

She thought about the travel times. Forty-five minutes in the Yukon and fifteen minutes or less in the helicopter. "Yes, fly. Call Mannie. I'll meet you in the kitchen."

When Roark came down, Jessica was on her second circle of the kitchen.

He joined her, helping in the only way he knew how, with his arm around her shoulders as she walked.

Five minutes later, Mannie ran into the kitchen. "Jessica, are you all right?"

She shook her head, as she was in the middle of a contraction. "No."

Roark turned to Mannie. "Is the 'copter ready?"

"Yeah, I'll see you out there." He ran back out into the morning air.

The sun was just coming up, which pleased Jessica immensely. She didn't relish the thought of flying in the dark, but she would, if needed. Taking the copter would cut their trip by two-thirds of the time, getting them there in fifteen minutes rather than forty-five. She didn't believe she had forty-five minutes left before this baby was born.

During the flight, Jessica heard Mannie on the radio.

"Bozeman Deaconess, Sullivan Air here, over."

"This is Bozeman Deaconess. What's your emergency? Over."

"We're bringing in Mrs. Sullivan, who's ready to have her baby. Over."

"Understood, Sullivan Air. We'll be ready when you arrive. What is your ETA? Over."

"We are ten minutes out, over."

"Okay, we're preparing for you now. Over."

"Thanks. Sullivan Air, over and out."

Roark rubbed her back. "Did you hear, Jessica? Just ten minutes, you can do it. Just hang on for a few more minutes, love."

Jessica started breathing again. She had to remember to breathe when she had a contraction, not hold her breath. It was hard to remember. The natural thing to do seemed to be to hold her breath.

Three contractions later, they were landing at the hospital.

They'd barely hit the ground when hospital personnel opened the door and helped her out onto a gurney.

Roark kept pace beside her as they ran, pushing the bed into the hospital's ER. They took her immediately to the elevator through the outer room of the ER with its green walls. She couldn't see it, but she would bet the floor was pale yellow linoleum. He looked down at Jessica on the gurney and smiled. "We're here. You made it, sweetheart. You made it."

"Oww." She reached for her belly, unable to put her thoughts into words. That was just as well, as her thoughts were angry ones. Where was the birthing room with its soft eggshell walls and brown speckled carpet?"

The doctor came out wearing green scrubs and a green hat. She had round glasses. "I'm Doctor Gable. I'll be helping you deliver your baby today." She looked up at Roark. "Has she had any problems with this pregnancy?"

"No. It's been textbook from the beginning. Her ob-gyn has been thrilled with her and her progress.

"Oww," Jessica moaned. She felt her body stretching as the baby moved downward. She felt a burning sensation as the baby kept moving down. "Where is Doctor Murtaugh?" She thought the doctor's glasses looked like the ones John Lennon wore. It didn't give her a lot of confidence in the poor doctor.

She checked her watch. "She couldn't make it in time. I was already here. And it looks like you got here just in time. Her contractions are just under two minutes. She'll be having the baby at any time. Are you attending the birth with your wife?"

"Yes, I am."

"Let's get you some scrubs. Nurse!"

"Yes, Doctor."

"I need Mr. Sullivan dressed in scrubs, a hat, and mask."

"Come with me, Mr. Sullivan," said the nurse.

He leaned down and kissed Jessica's forehead. "I'll be right back."

She nodded. "Fine." Jessica knew she sounded angry, but she was. This was all his fault.

Once in the delivery room, they removed her dress and covered her with a sheet and a warm blanket. The room itself wasn't anything like the birthing room they'd showed her. "Why aren't we in the birthing room? They promised me a soft tranquil experience with soft music, things that are relaxing to me." Instead, this room was non-descript. More green walls, no windows. And there had to be three nurses along with the doctor and some man she assumed was an anesthesiologist.

Dr. Gable looked down at her. "I'm sorry Jessica. Another mother already occupies the birthing room. According to your records here on the computer," the doctor looked at a laptop screen. "You thought you'd be camping this weekend. I understand someone you know is familiar with that. Though I can't imagine going camping when you're this pregnant."

Jessica rested between contractions. "It was a joke. I wouldn't go even seven months pregnant. It would be too uncomfortable."

"Would you like a warm blanket?"

"Thank you, I am cold. Why are these rooms always

so cold?" She took a deep breath and then shivered as she rubbed her arms above the blanket."

The doctor, whose manner never wavered and was always kind, looked at her. "It used to be done hoping it would prevent infections. However, now, it's for the comfort of the physician and his staff."

"I understand. It's got to be hard work to deliver a baby for someone for hours at a time. Never knowing if the baby will come quickly or slowly, be breech or have other distress. I couldn't do your job. It would be too stressful."

"It is, but it's also very rewarding to see a new life come into the world. Do you need another blanket?"

"Yes, that would be nice."

"All right, we'll get you a blanket." Doctor Gable signaled to someone. "In the meantime, I want to see what is happening down there. Raise your knees so we can put your feet in the stirrups."

Roark entered the room and came over to her. He leaned down and kissed her forehead. "How are you?"

She looked up at him and thought he looked like a hot doctor in the scrubs. "I'm sweaty and in pain. How do you think I am?"

"I know how you are and you can yell at me as much as you want. Doctor Murtaugh said you would want to." He took her right hand in his. "Squeeze my hand if it helps."

Just then another pain did hit, and she squeezed his hand as hard as she could. She wanted to push so badly.

The doctor sat at the bottom of the bed, which was

open with no footboard. Then Doctor Gable lowered the back a little and raised the foot a little.

"Jessica, you're at ten centimeters, and I need you to push now. Push hard. Let's get this baby out to meet its parents."

Less than an hour later, Colin Ross Sullivan was born.

The doctor laid him on Jessica's belly while the umbilical cord finished pulsing. When it was done, the doctor clamped off the cord and then cut it. After which they took him, weighed him—eight pounds and three ounces—and cleaned him.

A nurse brought him back, swaddled tight and with a little blue stocking cap on his head.

Jessica immediately unwrapped him and checked under his little hat. He had lots of curly coal black hair. She put his hat back on.

He was beautiful. The most beautiful baby she'd ever seen. He was long—twenty-one inches—but he was a good weight and so wasn't skinny like some babies are.

"Oh, Roark. Look at him, he's so…so perfect. How did we make such a perfect little being?"

Roark kissed the top of her head.

She tipped her head back and looked at him, her heart full of love for him and now for Colin.

He kissed her lips. "Thank you."

"For what?"

Roark had a small smile, and yet she'd never seen him more serious. "For marrying me and making me the happiest man alive. And then, when I thought I could never be happier than we were, you gave me this handsome little part of you and me who I don't think I could love more than I do." He kissed her again. "Thank you."

"Oh, Roark." She reached up and cupped his beloved face. "I should be the one thanking you. You made me whole...at least I thought you did, but now..." she looked down at Colin. "Now, I think this little man has made us both whole. And you're right. I don't think I could love him more than I do, but I know I will. Just as I love you more today than yesterday."

The nurses were all still there. One cleaning equipment used in the birth. Another cleaning the equipment used to clean and weigh Colin.

The doctor was there delivering the afterbirth.

Jessica knew this because of the research she'd done for her new contemporary western series.

Roark laid one arm across the top of the bed and, dwwwwwwith the other, he reached down and cupped her cheek. "I do you, too."

Suddenly, a tiny cry sounded.

She looked down into Colin's little face, which was all screwed up and angry. "I think he's hungry."

A nurse appeared. "Do you need help nursing the first time?"

Jessica laughed. "I don't know. It's the first time."

Roark chuckled.

The nurse did, too.

"Okay, while you feed him, I'll get you all cleaned

up. First, though, let's get him started nursing. I want you to put him in the crook of your elbow with his head close to your nipple. Then I want you to rub his lips with your nipple and encourage him a little until he latches on. It's instinctive for him to nurse, so you should just have to tease him and get him started."

Jessica did what she said and teased him.

He tried, latched on, and then lost it.

She enticed him again, and this time, it seemed to work.

"Very good," said the nurse. "You're a natural."

Roark stood beside her and watched her nurse. "I'm so proud of you. You gave birth to him like he was your tenth child, not your first."

Her eyes widened and her brows went up. "I am not having ten children. If you insist on that many kids, we'll adopt."

He laughed. "I'm not proposing you have that many children. I suggest we see how we do with this little mite before we plan on having more."

She let out a breath and relaxed. "Thank you. You had me worried for a moment."

"No worries, my love. We'll take all this slow and learn as we go. We have outstanding teachers in our parents. I'm sure they will be more than happy to answer any questions we have."

"That's true. We are so blessed. I love you, Roark Sullivan."

"I love you, too, Jessica Sullivan. Forever."

"And a day." She pulled him down for a kiss that was punctuated by a tiny cry.

"I think he wants to be involved." She lifted him and kissed one cheek.

Roark kissed the baby's other cheek.

And then they kissed each other.

The happiest family.

In Denver, an old Romany woman laughed with glee.

ALSO BY CYNTHIA WOOLF

The Prescott Brides

A Bride for Ross (Available in German)

A Bride for Frank

A Bride for Tucker

A Bride for Clay

A Bride for Brodie

* * *

Billionaire Cowboys

Her Secret Cowboy Billionaire (Available in German)

Her Mysterious Cowboy Billionaire (Available in German)

Her Royal Cowboy Billionaire (Available in German)

Her Christmas Cowboy Billionaire (Available in German

Her Bachelor Cowboy Billionaire

* * *

Heart Wish series

Heart of Stone

Heart of Shadow

Heart of Silver

* * *

Bachelors and Babies

Carter

* * *

Cupids & Cowboys

Lanie

* * *

Brides of Golden City

A Husband for Victoria

A Husband for Cordelia

A Husband for Adeline

* * *

The Brides of Homestead Canyon

A Family for Christmas

Kissed by a Stranger

Thorpe's Mail Order Bride

* * *

The Marshal's Mail Order Brides

The Carson City Bride

The Virginia City Bride

The Silver City Bride

The Eureka City Bride

Bride of Nevada

Genevieve

Brides of the Oregon Trail

Hannah

Lydia

Bella

Eliza

Rebecca

Charlotte

Amanda

Emma Rose

Nora

Opal

Brides of San Francisco

Nellie

Annie

Cora

Sophia

Amelia

Violet

Brides of Seattle

Mail Order Mystery

Mail Order Mayhem

Mail Order Mix-Up

Mail Order Moonlight

Mail Order Melody

Brides of Tombstone

Mail Order Outlaw

Mail Order Doctor

Mail Order Baron

Central City Brides

The Dancing Bride

The Sapphire Bride

The Irish Bride

The Pretender Bride

* * *

Destiny in Deadwood

Jake

Liam

Zach

* * *

Hope's Crossing

The Stolen Bride

The Hunter Bride

The Replacement Bride

The Unexpected Bride

* * *

Matchmaker & Co Series

Capital Bride

Heiress Bride

Fiery Bride

Colorado Bride

Troubled Bride

* * *

The Surprise Brides

Gideon

* * *

Tame

Tame a Wild Heart

Tame a Wild Wind

Tame a Wild Bride

Tame A Honeymoon Heart

Tame Boxset

* * *

Centauri Series (SciFi Romance)

Centauri Dawn

Centauri Twilight

Centauri Midnight

* * *

Singles

Sweetwater Springs Christmas

STAY CONNECTED!

Newsletter

Sign up for my <u>newsletter</u> and get a free book.

Follow Cynthia

https://www.facebook.com/cindy.woolf.5
https://twitter.com/CynthiaWoolf
http://cynthiawoolf.com

Don't forget if you love the book, I'd appreciate it if you could leave a review at the retailer you purchased the book from.

Thanks so much,
Cynthia

ABOUT THE AUTHOR

Cynthia Woolf is a USA Today Bestselling Author and an award-winning author of sixty-four historical western romance novels, two time-travel western romance novels, three contemporary western romance novels, one contemporary western novella and six sci-fi romance novels, which she calls westerns in space.

Along with these books she has also published five boxed sets of her books. The Tame Series, Destiny in Deadwood, The Marshals Mail Order Brides, The Brides of the Oregon Trail series, Centauri Series and Swords and Blasters.

Cynthia loves writing and reading romance. Her first western romance Tame A Wild Heart was inspired by the story her mother told her of meeting Cynthia's father on a ranch in Creede, Colorado. Although Tame A Wild Heart takes place in Creede that is the only similarity between the stories. Her father was a cowboy, not a bounty hunter, and her mother was a nursemaid (called a nanny now), not the owner of the ranch.

Cynthia credits her wonderfully supportive husband Jim and her great critique partners for saving her sanity and allowing her to explore her creativity.

Made in the USA
Middletown, DE
08 June 2023

32288085R00126